kisses & stones

A Playlist Kinda Love Story, Side A

d. allyson howlett

sensitive content warning
this book contains scenes of both verbal and slightly physical relationship / domestic abuse.
Please seek help from a trusted source, if needed.

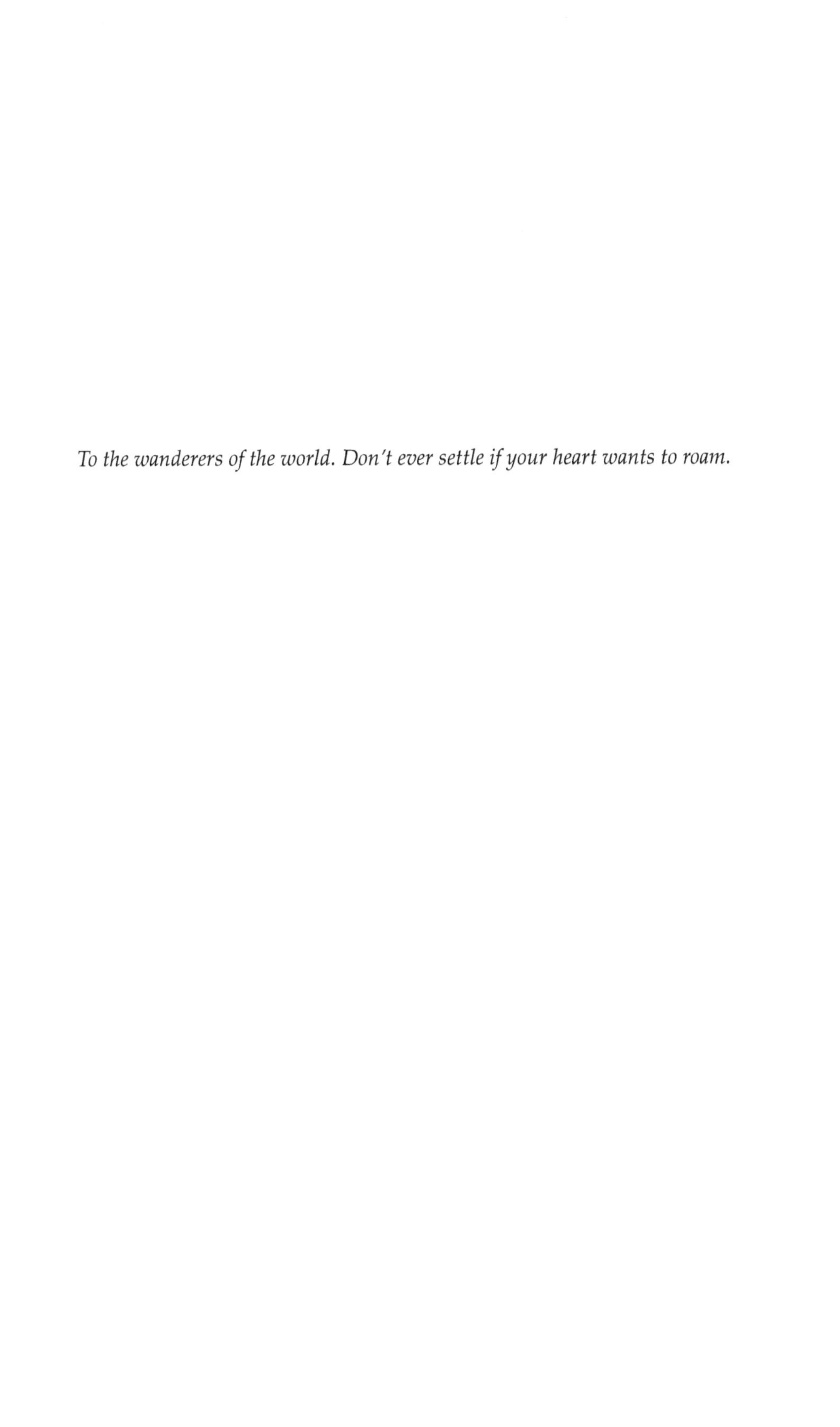

To the wanderers of the world. Don't ever settle if your heart wants to roam.

kisses & stones

one

. . .

IF THERE WAS anything I learned about high school gossip, it was that most of it started in the locker room. Words bounced off the cream painted walls, hitting every guy who would listen until it was too late. I didn't know why Chris thought it was a good idea to tell Logan and me his parents were away for the weekend. That was the biggest open party invitation anyone could ask for in high school. He basically announced on the loudspeaker that anyone who wanted an excuse to get wasted, high, and make out could do so at his parentless house.

I had to be there, if for nothing else, to witness Chris' reaction to all the uninvited guests he had unknowingly welcomed to his house.

It was cold as hell out. Pulling my hood up over my messy dirty blonde mop, I shoved my hands deep inside the pocket wells of my sweatshirt. I had my skateboard shoved in my black backpack. The streets were lined with cars, as usual. A train rattled against the tracks, echoing a metallic song through the air. I could see the tall iron legs of the bridge leading up to the platform in the distance. Cars, traveling east and west up North Broadway, omitted a dull hum as they rushed by.

My phone was blowing up, vibrating with the Mario power-up

sound every five seconds. Shooting it out, I could tell Chris' little open invite on Wednesday was well received.

> Pete, where R U!?

> Holy shit, something just broke.

> Ur coming late on purpose aren't u.

> GET HERE NOW!

I smiled to myself at his sheer desperation texts. Chris was such a nice guy, he couldn't tell people to get the fuck out.

Another buzz popped up on my screen.

> Chris is a fuckin' wreck and ur missin' it 😂

Logan. He was probably lounging on the couch with some girl, just watching Chris panic out all over the house. I am sure Logan tried to calm the situation, but once Chris hit his apex in the realm of anxiety, it was hard to knock him down.

> I'm a few blocks away. Tell Chris not to jump off the roof yet.

I stuffed my phone back in my pocket and continued on, closing the gap between me and Chris' house. This was a town that never slept, like most towns in the suburbs of New York. Living in the crosshairs of Old Country Road and one of the busiest malls on the island, Hicksville was pretty bustling with plenty of things to do and places to go. The noise of the massive train station might have bothered most people, but it was like a lullaby to me. Rattling iron wheels and the blaring horn, the squeak of the breaks as it stopped at the station, even the melodic double note of the sliding doors opening and closing. I realized it was something I would miss when I got older, something I took for granted because it had been part of my life for so long.

I made it down the street and crossed underneath the train tracks. There was a lot of angry yelling going on the other side, the side I needed to be on. Adjusting my glasses a bit, I slowed as I crossed the line of two people, obviously getting ready to kill each other. It wasn't until I was squarely across from them thatI realized who they were.

Every school had a quintessential bad boy or bad girl. At least that was what all the teen movies want you to believe. If I was going by the high school textbook definition, Ashley Carter was ours. From what I could make out, she had her hood up, her kinky light brown hair escaping from the sides around her face. She was walking away from someone wearing an unbuttoned plaid shirt and a mean look.

"Don't you walk away from me!" The voice of Westley De La Cruz thundered into the night.

He and Ashley were the power couple in our sophomore year, him being a senior to our younger selves. That reputation continued even after he graduated and grew into an entire mountain of heavy shit.

Ashley didn't turn around as her boots crashed onto the sidewalk like a stone giant. "I'll walk away from you whenever the fuck I feel like it!"

With my head down, I walked faster to get out of there. I needed to cross the street, but I could do so farther down without having to be within 100 feet of them.

"I own you!" There was a brief sound of a struggle. "Hey! Come back here!" Wes bellowed.

Their voices never faded, they just kept getting louder and louder. My pace slowed. Biting my lip, I fumbled with the little balls of string attached to the inside pocket of my sweatshirt. I had to mind my business and ignore them. Ashley, I was sure, could handle herself, but…

"Don't touch me, asshole!" she shrieked.

"Fuck you! Next time I see you talking to that shit for brains, I'm gonna slap some sense into you!"

I didn't know why I looked back, but dammit, I did. His hand shot out like a whip, grabbing Ashley by her jacket. Ashley's head jerked backward as he twisted her arm around to face him.

With an angry sneer, Ashley looked far from scared. "You'd never lay a fucking hand on me because you're a coward!"

Even from across the street, I felt the intense seething, equivalent to the fires of Mount Doom, radiating from Westley's body as he stood over her.

"What did you just call me?"

Dammit.

What I was about to do was suicide. With a deep breath, I stopped mid-walk. I wasn't thinking rationally at all, but I couldn't just walk away. Since there was no oncoming traffic, I plodded across the street until I was right by Ashley's side. I grabbed her arm and jerked it away from him, taking a stand between them.

"What the fuck," the words filtered out of Ashley's mouth like a whisper. She didn't pull away, and I wasn't about to turn around and look her in the eye. Not when I had Doomsday in front of me.

"Who the *fuck* are you?" Westley rushed me, my face hidden under my hood.

"Back off." I somehow said, the adrenaline pumping through my veins like a terrible reaction to Kryptonite.

"What did you say to me?"

I pushed my hood off my head and attempted a stone-cold expression, the best I could muster. I had to at least pretend I had some sort of control over my actions, but Westley scared the shit out of me. His gel caked hair hung down like straggly curtains against his tan buffed skin. His nostrils flared as the corner of his lip twitching into his clean-cut sideburns.

"Leave her alone."

His dark eyes got real wide, taking deep aggravated breaths. "Who the fuck are you to tell me what to do?"

"No one, honestly." I held in any panic that was trying to escape through my voice.

"I could knock your fucking teeth in, you know that?"

"Yeah, you could and would be marvelously successful at it."

He glanced at Ashley for a moment. "Is this one of your fuck buddies, Ash?"

"Fuck you, Wes!" She sprang off her toes at the force of her words.

"I don't know her, okay," My body tensed to hold back any uncontrollable shaking. "I mean, I know of her, but… you shouldn't be yelling at her like that."

"How do you know, you little prick?"

His breath was hot and riddled with that musty cigarette smell.

"Just back off."

I kept eye contact with him by some unexplained miracle. Maybe there was some hidden Bruce Banneresque power within me, just waiting to rear its ugly green head. Or I was out of my mind.

He swiped my glasses right off my face, causing me to wince and take a step back. "First, I'll break these." He folded the arms of my frames into a fist. "Then I'll break you."

I could make out the blurred lines of his profile, but barely. What the hell was I thinking? My life was about to come to a swift end. Sweat began to build up against the sleeves of my jacket.

"What's the matter, Wes? This nobody making you feel small? For fuck's sake, you're such an asshole."

Ashley's interjection sent a jolt of surprise down my spine. His reaction was lost to me, but his head tilted up, like he was looking behind me.

"You shut the hell up!"

The blur of his face came back to semi-view. With a scoff, he threw my glasses back at me, and my delayed reaction caused them to fall onto the sidewalk.

"She's right. You're a nobody. Not worth shit." Westley moved closer so that long drawn out scowl was clear as day in my distorted vision. "If I ever see you again, you little fucker, it's open season."

He glared behind me, pointing with a sharp finger. "You got off easy, but this isn't over, Ash."

Brushing past us, he crossed the street with an angry stride, his fists balled against his sides. I waited until I couldn't hear his footsteps anymore, allowing myself to breathe again.

What the hell happened? Was that even me, or was my body snatched for the last minute of my adolescent life?

Ashley's arm slowly fell away from my hand as my grip loosened to fumble around for my glasses.

"What the fuck is wrong with you?"

Her feet crunched against the ground as she came around. Her curly locks blinded my already blurred vision as she squatted down and shoved my glasses into my hands. From what I could make out, there were a few scuffs and scratches on the lenses, but nothing a good buffering wouldn't take care of. After placing them back on, I could finally see again. One arm was loosely resting on my ear, but hopefully no one would notice.

Ashley was standing over me, her hands at her hips, looking almost as menacing as Westley. I stood, fixing the position of my frames. "Are you all right?"

There was tension in her tawny face, her hair wildly crimped on both sides, which made her expression even more intense. Despite how she was holding herself, her clear hazel eyes darted back and forth with uncertainty, searching for some sort of explanation. Either I was crazy or I rationally stuck up for her. Me, a complete nobody. She probably didn't even know what my name was.

"You got a death wish or something?"

"Are you all right?" I repeated, only because I had no clue what else to say.

"You're lucky I saved your ass. Next time, mind your own damn business." She backed away before turning tail, leaving me standing alone with my hands still shaking from the aftershock of the moment. Waiting for only a few seconds more, I pulled my hood up again.

"You're welcome." I yelled after her half-heartedly.

It was hard to keep the Hulk adrenaline from pumping through my body, and it was causing my feet to move faster than my thoughts could comprehend.

As I continued on, I planned on keeping my mouth shut about this incident. This was fuel for rumor fodder. I could pull an amalgamation of hundreds of situations and circumstances from this and fabricate them into about a dozen spin-off series at once. Anything that involved Ashley, no matter who you were, was grounded for immediate publication.

I was only a few houses away from Chris. From the sound of it, the party was in full swing. No sirens or flashing lights, so that was a good sign, or bad. Frankly, I didn't know which situation was worse. The muffled music and voices were expanding in volume as I drew closer. The sounds shook some sense into my panicked mind, clearing away the unnecessary bullshit that had injected itself like a brain slug trying to take over.

I did the right thing, and no one had to realize that but me. Sure, it was nice to be appreciated for your accolades, but this was not one of those situations where that would happen, and so what? Ashley clearly had control over him, if all she had to do was say I was worthless for Wes to not permanently cripple me. And she seemed okay, stunned, but okay. I hope she didn't find him again, but she didn't seem the type to run after a guy, begging for forgiveness. Not her.

Wes said he'd kill me if he ever saw me, something I would positively abide by. Even used a line from good ol' Kreese, though I doubt he was aware of it. He didn't seem like a Cobra Kai fan, though he'd fit right in.

The house was swarming, but not as bad as I imagined. A half-dozen people were standing on his front porch, socializing as music pulsed from the open windows. I didn't recognize them, so they must have been from another school. They moved aside as I passed them to reach the door. Before I even turned the knob, Chris was there, coming at me like a last surviving man off a mountain expedition gone wrong.

"Pete! Holy shit," Chris practically dragged me into the house, "what took you so long!?"

His dark eyes were frantic, a light glaze of sweat sat where his brown skin met his fro-line.

I shrugged, pulling my hood off my head. "I got held up."

"Your girl's looking for you too." he said as I passed through the door. "So get your ass in here!"

My mind was unable to shift from one girl to the next, with Ashley still fresh on my mind. I hoped to god I didn't show it.

two

. . .

"WHY DOES this kind of shit always happen to me?" Chris whispered under this breath, pressing his hands on either side of his head.

His frantic eyes darted from one person to the next as undesirables infested his living room. Music was blaring above the average decibels the human ear should endure. The open concept layout of his house gave the perfect 360 degree view of the living room, kitchen, and back deck, which were already teaming with people.

"Word gets out..." was the only lackluster replay Logan could give.

As I put a somewhat comforting hand on Chris' shoulder, Logan tapped on his stereotypical red cup with his surfer blonde hair falling into his face. Chris was rubbing the sides of his head so hard I thought his fingers would fall off, the palms of his hands almost white against the darkness of his skin.

"Lesson learned," I butted matter-of-factly, "do not announce your parents will be away for the weekend unless you are 100% clear of all no good party goers."

"Should we call the cops?" Chris asked.

"To your own house?" Logan shook his head. "Are you crazy?"

"It's your house. Tell them to leave," I added.

"I can't do that." Chris sat up from the green marbled island in the middle of his once picturesque Martha Stewart kitchen.

"Why not?" I questioned, with my eyes squinting behind my glasses.

"I don't know… I… I think I need some air."

"You really want to go outside to that?" Logan gestured toward the back of the house to where the sliding doors housed the spill over of people in the backyard.

"At least tell them to turn the music down." I stepped away from the island. "Then there is less of a chance of some neighbors' getting finger happy on their phones."

"What?" Chris asked.

"9-1-1. The easiest number to dial." Logan smiled as he turned to me.

"Shut up! You are not helping me feel any better!"

It was cruel to make fun of the situation but oh so entertaining. Chris made it so easy to rip on him. He was too nice compared to Logan and me. Logan was a getting-used-to kind of friend. A typical California skater mentality on him, he even looked the part with his overall chill expression. The only difference was we weren't in California, we lived in New York.

Groaning, Chris rose from his mini-breakdown. "This was just supposed to be us wasting time playing Smash Brothers or some shit."

"Well, it's definitely some shit," I replied.

A loud crash came from down the hall. Chris hopped on his feet. "What the hell was that?"

"I don't know." Logan shrugged, taking a sip of whatever he was drinking. "But it didn't sound good."

"If anything breaks in this house, I swear to god…" Chris moved like a bullet down the hallway, his fists clenched to keep himself composed.

"You better go with him to make sure he doesn't punch anyone," I said.

Moving the cup away from his mouth, Logan looked at me. "Why don't you go?"

"I want to find Mari. Chris said she was looking for me."

"Ah." He smirked. "Last I saw her she was outside."

He backed away into the crowd of bodies that Chris disappeared into. "Good luck trying to find her in this mess." And with that, he made his way with unnatural ease down the hallway.

My gaze darted from the front door to the back. With a deep breath, I made my way toward the glass sliding door leading onto the deck. Chris had one of those places where no one lived behind him, so no homes to shadow his own. That was a blessing in disguise on a night like tonight. Not that there weren't houses on either side, houses on top of houses with maybe a small square of space in between for grass to grow.

I slipped through the crowd, grazing rather than push. I didn't know anyone here really, except for our immediate core group of friends and some guys from the high school baseball team Chris and I played on since freshman year. Everyone else had familiar faces that I'd seen in yearbooks and team photos that lined the school hallways.

As I reached the double doors leading to the backyard, a flash of kinky brown hair brushed past my line of sight. My heart jumped into my throat. Had Ashley followed me here? My brief panic only lasted a second, because the person attached to the hair turned to the side, showing off a pointy nose and a face full of freckles. Definitely not Ashley.

My nerves were still on edge, even with so much distracting me. A tall rectangular mirror hung to the right of the doors. Dragging my fingers through my hair again, there was barely any pomade left to hold it back. I adjusted the straps on my backpack, too afraid to let it out of my sight. I took off my glasses and rubbed my prescriptions against my sweatshirt.

With a deep breath, I slipped them back on and stepped onto the deck. There was a nice fire pit right off of it, which sat about four feet away from the fence. I didn't really have to search before I heard a voice call my name.

"Pete, thank god!" Before I could turn around, Mari had her arms around me. Her long dark hair wafted the scent of coconut creme in my direction. She planted a forceful kiss against my unexpecting lips. But damn, if I didn't bask in the 2.3 milliseconds it lasted.

"Hey," I replied, wrapping my arms around her waist.

"This is beyond insane." Rina stepped next to us with her arms folded and green eyes squinting with disdain.

"I blame Logan for this," Mari said, leaning into me a little.

I let out a lighthearted snort. "Is this the first time in 2 years you're not blaming me for something?"

Her dark tresses lying straight against her olive skin were captivating. She wasn't petite, like Rina, but shapely in all the right ways.

"You and I both know it was Logan," she reiterated.

I shook my head, "Nah, this resulted from Chris' big mouth in the locker room."

"Where are those two, anyway?" Rina asked, moving in closer so she didn't have to yell.

"Struggling to prevent bodily damage to the house," I breathed out.

"I can't be here anymore, I have to get out of here." Mari shuddered. "All these people are making me sick to my stomach."

"Because they look repulsive or…"

Mari pushed me. "You're the only vile thing here."

"Ouch, that wasn't nice."

She looked at me, eyebrow raised and the corner of her lip turned up into her cheek. I could never tell if she was goofing around or serious anymore. It's like someone kept playing with a light switch in my mind, deciding whether it should put me off.

"Well, are you going to walk me home or not?" she said after a beat of silence.

"You are not leaving me here," Rina interjected.

"I would never leave you anywhere, Rina."

Groaning to myself, I looked back at the house, still regurgitating people and swallowing them back up again. "I don't think Chris will let me leave."

"Just make up some excuse. Say I don't feel good, which isn't entirely untrue."

Turning back to her, I realized I didn't have a choice. It wasn't that, but I hated bailing on a friend in a dire situation. And this was a dire situation.

"All right," I replied. "Meet me out front."

"Thank God." Mari whisked past me.

"Thanks, Pete. We owe you one," Rina spoke with a sigh of relief.

I waited for them to push through the bodies of people before moving back inside to search for Chris. I couldn't just disappear without him knowing. His dark mini fro stuck out from the crowd. Bent over, Chris was picking up something that looked semi-destroyed.

"Hey," I called, and he looked up to me, "Mari's not feeling good so I'm going to take her home."

"No," he stood up quick, grabbing my arm ready to plead, "you are not leaving."

"I won't be gone long. Plus, Logan's around here… somewhere."

"Yeah, making out with god knows who in the basement." He rolled his eyes, shaking his hands free of all the suckery this night had been.

"I'll be right back. She lives like five minutes away."

"Fine, fine." He waved me off. "Go. Leave in my most critical hour of need."

He went back to picking up the shattered pieces of something; it looked like it used to be a glass plate or figurine, something his parents would notice was absent once they came back.

"Maybe I'll call the cops on my way back to save you the trouble of waiting for someone else to do it."

His eyes grew enormous as he looked back at me, "Don't even think about it."

✼

"So where are you applying to?" Rina's voice caught me off guard as we walked along the sidewalk toward Mari's house. As we ran across the street where I, less than 30 minutes ago, had jumped in front of the raging bull that was Westley De La Cruz, a shudder ran down my spine. Luckily, it was cold enough to play it off as being affected by the weather, in case anyone asked why my arms tensed up.

"What?"

"College," she said, unconcerned about my momentary lapse in attention. "Where do you plan on applying?"

"I… I don't know."

"April is around the corner," Mari added sharply. "You need to get serious about this kind of stuff, Pete."

"Yeah, yeah."

Mari rolled her eyes. "Come on, Pete! You don't want to let this lie."

"You're smart enough to get in anywhere," Rina added. "I don't think Mr. Kane has had a better student than you in Physics class."

College, another thing on my proverbial to-*not*-do list. All the encouragement in the world couldn't push me to favor one over another. I had no clue what the hell I wanted to do after high school. It just seemed so big and let me tell you, bigger is not always better.

I liked how things were in high school. My routines were on point, and life was pretty much on cruise control. College was this giant road block that I couldn't see myself getting around, but everyone was dragging me by my hair to do it. It wasn't like deciding what flavor of ice cream to get from the Mr. Softee truck.

"It's a big decision, you know? I don't want to just apply anywhere."

"I get that, but you're running out of time." Mari nudged my side. "Get to it before it's too late."

"I don't think my parents will forget, trust me."

We crossed the street, our feet scraping against the cracked blacktop. Heavy, looming shadows cast over us as we passed under the train tracks. Mari's house was down the block from here.

Hurrying along, we made it onto her street. Her house was massive, smack dab in the middle of the half a mile long stretch of block. It stuck out like a king amongst beggars. Her parents had poured a ton of money into making it a trophy house that told anyone walking by, "Hey, we earned this."

Built of sandy brick, it had one of those fancy metal roofs. Two giant stone pillars framed the enormous front door which was two-fold with small stain glass windows flanking each side. Well kept bushes lined the front porch and the sandstone, or whatever stone pathway that met us at the cracked sidewalk, could be compared to the yellow brick road from Oz.

"Thanks for walking us back, Pete." Rina waved and made her way toward the front door.

Mari looked at me as she took my hand. "You going back to Chris'?"

"I have to. I told him I would."

"You're a good friend." She kissed me gingerly on the lips. "Call you tomorrow?"

"Yeah," I said, wishing she would've kissed me a little longer. It was cold, sure, but that could have warmed me up for the walk back.

"Let me know what happens." Before she turned down the front path, she paused, doing a double take with her eyes narrowing a bit. "Your glasses are crooked."

"What?" I swore my heart stopped as I grabbed them off my face and looked at them like it surprised me. Mari took them from me, carefully bending off of the arms in between her fingers.

"This one is loose." Her eyes fell back to me. "When did that happen?"

"Oh," I breathed, swallowing the dry lump in my throat. "I dropped them on the way here. Hit the curb with my board."

"And they fell off? How hard did you hit?"

"I stumbled and they kind of got away from me. But thank you. Your concern for my glasses physical well-being is duly noted."

"Hmm." She handed them back to me. "Make sure you fix that. They're more likely to fall off again."

"Got it." I slipped my frames back on my face, focusing in on her small, sweet smile.

"See ya." She slipped away from me and walked to the door where Rina was waiting. As it opened, Mari's dad peeked his small, disgruntled head out into the chill of the night.

Not wanting to seem like I didn't notice him, I lifted my hand to wave. "Hi, Mr. Khatri."

With his usual scowl, he let the girls slip past him as he closed the door. I was never sure if that was his way of saying hello or fuck off.

Me not being Indian, just a European mutt, didn't sit well with his high standards of the guys his only daughter should spend her time with.

Drawing a deep breath, letting it plume over my head, I turned on the heels of my Airwalks and made my way back toward Chris' house. That was a close one. I should have known that Mari was too observant to overlook an insignificant detail like my glasses tilting slightly. I hated that I had to lie, but it was better than the alternative. She would blow her stack clear off if she knew what shenanigans I was up to just before getting to Chris'. Full-blown, Mt. Vesuvius level clearing.

My thoughts turned back to the whole scenario with Westley. I could still smell his musty smokers breath. This would not be a sleep it off kind of experience, something you just forget after a few hours. It's not like I played heroics very often, in fact never. It would take a while, but I just had to convince myself it never happened.

I wondered if Ashley made it home okay. I should have walked her home, if she'd let me. Probably not. She forgot all about it by now, so I should, too. I didn't understand why she told Wes to back off. Who was I to her? Just a nobody. Someone I am sure she had never noticed before tonight.

The time it took me to get here and back would be too long for Chris to handle, so I shot out my phone to send him a quick text, but he beat me to it.

> The cops are here. Don't come back.

Damn. Logan was still there, at least. What help he would be, hell if I knew.

three

· · ·

THEY MADE NO ARRESTS AT CHRIS' busted party, just a broken TV and a lot of shit to clean up. Luckily, any alcohol that was brought by outsiders left with them. Chris didn't fill me in on more than that. I'm sure his parents, having to come home early from wherever they were, didn't go over too well.

It was early afternoon the next day, and I stood over the never-depleting pile of crisp new comic books we got in the latest shipment. Logan stood there with a slouch, tossing around a wad of gum in his mouth. He worked here with me. Here meaning Grasshoppers, a small little rinky-dink comic book and collectibles shop nestled in one of the million strip malls across the island. I was a key holder here. The only guy Dave, the absentminded owner of this place, could trust with such a responsibility.

The shop was snug, but it was a wall to wall nerd paradise. Comics ran up and down the four small aisles from floor to ceiling. Large towering rectangle shelves stood in each corner, piled high with figurines, key chains and all other manner of comic book related geek-dom. The ceiling housed two fans and a huge life-size replica of Super-man, crashing in from the sky with his cape blowing in the make believe wind. His arm outstretched, ready to deliver swift justice to the villains that dared walk the aisles of the store.

It was pretty sweet, coming into work every week with the chiseled jaw of Clark Kent to greet you. The job wasn't a gold mine. In fact, I got paid shit for the work I did here. But I loved this place. I'd probably work here for free if Dave asked me to.

I got Logan a job here about a year ago. Logan was exactly how he looked. Lazy. But he was an attaché of comigraphy–totally made that one up–and fit in well with the overall mechanics of the job.

"Okay," Logan leaned against the counter with his arms folded, "Michael Keaton or Adam West?"

I scoffed, almost insulted. "Keaton. That's not even a debate."

"That's fair, that's fair. What about Keaton or Bale?"

Putting the pen down onto the clipboard, I shook my head. "I'm still going with Keaton."

"No, no fucking way. Bale could kick Keaton's ass in five minutes!"

"Okay, sure. Bale was a much more physically fit and athletic Batman. I don't deny that. But Keaton had Wayne's mentality down."

"What? No way. Bale set the bar." Logan shook his head, his hands raised in protest at the very notion that Keaton was a far superior Batman.

Pulling a freshly pressed stack of comics from the box, I moved over to the glass countertop and spread them out. "Think about it. Batman spent his entire life obsessing over his parent's death, hoping that, one day, he'd be able to take sweet revenge for the injustice that took them away from him. His entire life! No one could come out of that completely normal and sane. Keaton had the right idea, Wayne teetering on the edge of insanity, a self-absorbed, psychotic billionaire vigilante crime fighter who felt he was a better judge than justice."

I couldn't help but smile, sensing I had won this debate. "Batman had some serious demons, and Keaton was a genius at pulling that off."

My words seemed to get through his sun bleached hair. "Touché my friend."

"Do you even know what that word means?"

"Kind of.. Sort of…"

The bell jingled with foot traffic through the front door. I peeked up.

Ashley Carter, her curly hair barely touching her shoulders, walked into this temple of nerds with black buckled boots, jeans, and a dark blue hoodie. Stopping for a millisecond, she looked at me, her one eyebrow raised up against her forehead, before skipping down the aisle as if she were a regular here.

A faint streaking sound inched toward me as Logan's hands ran along the glass, sliding over in a whisper. "What the hell is Ashley Carter doing here?"

I shrugged, trying to ignore the sudden dread I felt building up in my throat. "How should I know?"

I went back to sorting through the merchandise, stashing new issues inside the rows of boxes we kept behind the counter. At least five would end up on the shelf, eventually. As soon as Ashley left, that is. I didn't want to skulk around the store while she was here.

Aside from Chris' party, Friday's events never happened. To open my mouth about it, wouldn't affect anyone but me. Plus, it was Ashley Carter. I didn't need another insane person breathing down my neck if I opened my mouth about it, not that I was afraid.

It was the right thing to do. If she wanted to run her mouth about it, that was her choice. A guy like me sticking up for her? The meanest, most controversial girl in school? The only one it would harm was me, and I was not the type of guy who required unwanted attention, or attention, period. I had my likes, dislikes, and respect from the only people I cared to get respect from. So, what did I have to worry about? She wouldn't ruin her reputation by being associated with me. A nobody who she probably didn't even know existed until Friday night. I aim to keep it that way as best I can.

"Excuse me!" her voice rang out from the back. "Can I get some help over here?"

I turned to Logan who gave me this deadpan stare, like he was about to face a whole slew of zombies empty handed. "You heard her."

Shaking his head, he exhaled quickly. "You can't be serious."

"Oh, I'm serious."

"Why can't –"

"Because I am technically the boss while Dave is not here, so... yeah. Sorry."

He took a deep breath before stepping away from the counter. I watched as he ambled toward the back, his eyes darting to me, hoping I would psyche him out and relieve him from this incredibly cruel but comical situation.

No dice man. I wouldn't even throw him initiative.

I resumed my duties, sorting and checking to make sure all the deliverables were in order. It wasn't long before I heard Logan come shuffling back, laying his hands on the counter and leaning across it toward me. "Dude," he stared, dumbfounded, "she wants you."

Just perfect. I set down my clipboard as not to seem out of my fucking mind, like I was willingly walking into a fist to the face. The surge of adrenaline I felt on Friday night didn't want to kick in, so I willed myself to act like this was something I did every day.

"Fine," I stepped away from the counter, "take over for me."

I couldn't even bring myself to face Logan. I was too afraid he'd see how nervous I was, even with my glasses on. Despite Logan's chillax attitude, he could read me like a book if he put the effort in. We've been friends forever, so it was hard not to know what the other was thinking in times like this.

It took all my focus to stop dragging my feet across the crudely carpeted floor. I kept my head up, the back of her in my line of sight at all times. When she sensed my approach, she turned around, those bright hazel eyes cutting clean through me. She had this know-it-all smirk on her face. I came up next to her, pushing my glasses up the bridge of my nose. "Yeah, what can I help you with today?"

I must have sounded like a square, but she didn't seem to care what I said or how I said it.

"You know that was really stupid what you did the other day," she stated so matter of fact. "Wes could have knocked you out."

"Well, he didn't..." I hesitated a moment, "you're welcome."

"What were you thinking, stepping in like that?"

"Apparently, I wasn't thinking at all. Next time I'll just let him hit you."

She casually glanced through the comics on the wall in front of us. "He'd never hit me."

"Keep telling yourself that." Eyebrows raised, Ashley turned as if she wasn't sure if I was serious or crazy. If I told my week-ago-self that I would have talked like this to Ashley Carter, I wouldn't believe I was sober. I wanted her to get the hell out of here, and her lack of appreciation was raising my aggression levels. I wasn't expecting her to bake me a cake, but a "thank you" would be nice. Ignoring her stare, I bit my lip and forced myself to gawk at the wall. "So, do you need anything comic related?"

She shifted in her stance, sighing in pretend frustration. "I've never read one of these things. Care to give me some recommendations?" She pulled at the corner of one issue, bending the crispness of its page ever so slightly. "And none of that spandex flying shit. If that's all ya got, don't waste my time."

"There's a lot more to comics than superheroes. You can find some pretty interesting stuff."

I scanned the rows of colorful images, big letters and flashy titles before coming across a rather simple, yet eye-catching issue. Reaching up, I plucked it from the shelf. "Here, this seems more your style."

Carefully, she took it from my hand and looked it over. "*Skydoll*?" she cringed with disgust. "What's this about?"

"It's a bunch of mini-stories created by different writers in distinct art styles. A little uncensored, erotic if you will."

"Uncensored and erotic?" Her dark brows raised again across her beige colored skin. "You think I'm erotic?"

"No," I replied forcibly, "but you seem like someone who would appreciate that kind of reading material."

"Is that so?" Experimenting with it in her hand, she flipped through the pages. I watched her expression change from snarky and smart to confused, like she was unsure of what to do. Her eyes fell to a colorful knitted bracelet around her wrist. She touched it gingerly, letting it slowly turn over to expose where it was tied. "I'm not really like that, you know."

"Like what?"

"What Wes said about me," she looked up, "I don't screw around like that."

She must have been talking about when Wes referred to me as her quote "fuck buddy". I knew what that was. I never had one myself, nor would I plan on having one, especially not Ashley. It's not that she wasn't pretty, she was… really pretty. And, standing this close to her, she smelled like spearmint. Like really strong gum, so aromatic I could taste it with every breath I took in her direction. I never looked at her in that way, or looked at her period. But now she was right in front of me, impossible to ignore.

"I never thought you did."

That uncertain expression on her face melted away in an instant. I wasn't lying. I really didn't think she was someone who slept around. I mean, you'd have to be Joker level crazy to cheat on Wes. And she didn't come across as someone with a death wish.

Closing the comic rather abruptly, she tilted her chin up. "All right, I'll take this."

"Sure."

Walking up to the register, she trailed a few feet behind me. Logan's gaze fell on us, practically foaming at the mouth to know the story behind this chance encounter. I tapped on the glass in front of him. "Ring her up, dude."

Ashley slid the issue his way, and he took it carefully from her. I walked back around the counter to return to my duties on stock. Logan was in such a trance. I don't think he blinked during that entire transaction. "Do you need a bag?"

"Nah," she shrugged while eyeing me, "I'm good."

I nodded. "Enjoy."

"I will," she took the comic and tucked it inside her jacket. "See you around, Pete."

We both watched her turn and walk toward the door with a sassy bounce in her step. As the door rang from her departure, Logan spun around to me with gigantic eyes. "What the fuck man, what the *fuck*?"

"What is wrong with you?" Shaking my head, I went back to work, wishing he would forget about this whole thing.

"Oh, come one! Ashley doesn't just decide, 'Hey, let me walk into this hole-in-the-wall comic book store on the ass end of town to say hi to my good friend Pete, who I have never spoken to or even breathed at before.' That just does not happen."

This would not go away. Once Logan got his focus on something, he was relentless. My heroics would not go untold after long with him poking around like an annoying fly. Why did she have to come in here?

"Let it go, man." I knew I couldn't shake him off, but I had to at least pretend.

"No, no way, you spill it! Come on, man!"

"All right," I tapped my fingers against the glass countertop, "but you need to promise me you won't tell anyone."

"Oh shit, did you cheat on Mari with Ashley?"

"No! Goddammit, no!" This was getting out of hand. Rarely did Logan keep a secret, but I was hoping this would afford him enough resolve to know not to spill his guts on me. He was one of my best friends. How I wish that meant something more now than ever.

I didn't regret what I did, but now, I was starting to. "Promise me you won't tell anyone."

"Yeah, yeah, I promise."

"All right." I took a deep breath, preparing myself for what I was about to do.

four

· · ·

I TAPPED my pen on my desk in history class as Chris hovered over me with that expected look on his face. I couldn't ignore him even if I tried, him and the 20+ other faces giving me odd glances and whispering under their breath. It was like that all morning. Weird looks and wide gasps had been circling me as I walked down the halls of stale blue lockers. This could only mean one thing. Somehow, word got out about my Friday night heroics. This was only first period, but I knew this would follow me for days and days…. And fucking days.

"So, is it true?" Chris leaned against the back of his chair, his fro-pick being the only thing I could stare at to keep myself level.

"Is what true?" I was over the explanations already, and they hadn't even started. Goddammit, if I found out that Logan was the one to open his big mouth…

"You and Ashley Carter."

"Great."

Chris jumped out of his seat. "So it is! Pete, what is wrong with you, man?"

I glanced at Rina, sitting one seat back across from us on the left, eyebrows turned in and lips pressed with concern. We were in the first row against the door side of the classroom. The generic black and white clock ticked away the last few seconds before the bell announced the start of class.

"That asshole boyfriend of hers was getting pretty physical, and not in a good way."

"So…" Chris' leg was bouncing up and down with anticipation.

"What was I supposed to do?" I shrugged. "Let her get the shit kicked out of her?"

"Dude, she is the definition of bad news, and *yes*! Walk the fuck away! I bet she could beat his ass anytime she wanted."

Other faces glanced our way as the secret, which clearly was not a secret, filtered from desk to desk.

Rina chimed in, "That was very admirable of you, Pete. Don't let him tell you it wasn't the right thing to do."

"Come on," I leaned back in my chair, "like you wouldn't have done the same thing?"

"Hell no! This is Ashley and Wes we're talking about! The guy's been arrested three times for God's sake!" Chris tried to lower his voice, but he was well past the ability to control it.

"That was for street racing." Rina flipped open her notebook to a blank page, readying for the start of class.

"Yeah, and beating the shit out of some guy for scuffing his Jordans!"

I shook my head. "That sounds made up."

"The point is, he is not someone you want to mess with. And getting between him and his girl is a recipe for disaster. A.k.a death."

"Pete," Rina leaned closer to us, "you have nothing to be ashamed of."

"Who said I was ashamed? What the hell are people saying?"

"All sorts of shit." Chris folded his arms. "None of it's true, of course, or… is it?"

"Whatever." The clock was winding down the final seconds. I was ready for this conversation to be over. "Let them say what they want. I did what I did and I don't care what people say."

"He's just being a jerk, don't listen to him." Rina settled back into her seat.

"I hope for his sake, it was worth it." Chris slid back down in his seat.

Rina's eyes widened, giving Chris a stare comparable to that of Medusa herself. "Don't make it worse, Chris. We're his friends, and it's our job to stick up for him. Besides," glancing back at me, her face much softer, "Ashley may not have a great reputation, but she's still a person."

"A snake more like it." Chris leaned forward in the back of his chair. "Did you hear what happened with her and Karson Schmitz?"

"He was in the hospital for appendicitis," Rina answered.

"That's what they *want* you to believe."

"By the way," I cut in, "how'd it go with your parents after their weekend was so rudely interrupted?"

Chris' face hardened in an instant. "Oh ha, ha, ha. Hilarious."

"If you're done with your riveting conversation," a booming voice turned all our heads back toward the front of the room, "we'd like to start class now."

Mr. Solosky stood with wrinkles in his forehead and a tight-lipped expression on his face. It made him look big, bigger than he already was. And I didn't mean fat. I meant tall and broad like a football player. He had to be at least six foot six, intimidating as hell for a retired cop. Weirdly enough, four out of the last five history teachers I've had were retired cops. I guess it was like an elective they could choose once they turned in their badge. Move to upstate New York and take up hunting or become a high school history teacher.

"Sorry, Mr Solosky," I said and settled back on my desk, pen in hand.

Class went on forever, that stupid sinking feeling never leaving my stomach. I wasn't looking forward to the rest of the school day. I had to see Mari at some point. What was she going to say about me helping Ashley?

As the bell rang, ending first period, I waited for most of our classmates to disperse before sliding out of my chair with books in hand.

Chris led the way into the flooded hallway. He turned around on his cleaned up Nike's facing me. "Are you coming to baseball tryouts?"

"I don't know," I mumbled, as I tried to ignore anyone who seemed more interested in me than usual.

"Come on, man, you're the best short-stop this school has! I'd hate to not have you on the team."

Chris was a prime example of a star athlete. He was popular without actually being popular, if you know what I mean. Everyone liked him and gave him tons of respect. We've been on the high school baseball team since freshman year, him being the catcher and team captain, and me on short-stop. This year, though, I wasn't feeling it. I was sure he'd convince me eventually, it'd be stupid of me not to.

"They're giving out two scholarships for baseball alone this year, you're top pick," he added as he pushed passed bodies to reach the crossroads of the senior hallway.

I sighed. "I'll have to think about it."

"Well, don't think too long." Chris backed away to the right. "See ya around."

Watching him disappear to his second period classroom, I took a deep breath and turned left down the hall, Rina falling in beside me. "What's wrong, Pete?" she asked. "You always look forward to tryouts."

"I don't know," I answered. "Guess I'm just messed up with all this after high school thinking."

She nodded as we walked together toward our next class. All of us were in honors at Hicksville High, and Rina, Chris and I practically shared the same schedule. Logan and Mari were on the track under us. Not that it made them any less intelligent. Mari was probably smarter than me, especially with music, but school was all about book smarts, which was complete bull. Not that it made transitioning to college any easier.

"It's a lot," Rina sighed, clutching her books closer to her chest. "My mom's had my applications ironed out and dry cleaned since September. She isn't giving me much of a choice on what schools I apply to."

"That sucks."

"It's not that bad. I probably would have applied to everywhere on her list, anyway. I need to focus on the best if I'm doing the whole doctor thing. But I'm not ready to think about it yet. I want to enjoy the last few months of high school before all the seriousness starts, ya know?"

"Yeah, I know." I moved out of the way of someone not paying any attention. "Where are you looking?"

"Mostly on the east coast. I can't imagine being too far from home." She shuddered a bit.

"Where did your parents go again?"

"Harvard."

I whistled. "I should have guessed that. I'm sure you're applying there, right?"

"Yeah."

"Once they get your application, they'll probably throw you a party just for considering them."

A shy smile stretched across her face. "What about you?"

"Nah," I shook my head, "I don't think I'm the Harvard type."

We reached the door to the physics lab. I slowed down, dragging my feet as we walked through the door. "Don't think too much about this Ashley thing," she said. "It will blow over in a few days. Later no one will even care to remember."

"We'll see, I guess."

I hated people giving unwanted attention to things that had no impact on their lives. All the head turns and odd glances I've had the pleasure of experiencing turned my good deed into a bad thing. Rina got it. Why couldn't everyone else? This made the fact that I hadn't talked to Mari about it even more gut twisting. Maybe I should have told her already. Then I wouldn't be going into this with doubts that it would cause our relationship to get worse.

She pushed my arm gingerly as she made her way toward the back of the classroom. Walking to the other side, past the rows of giant square tables with sinks shining clean in the center, I sat down on the dark brown stool of my assigned station. My fellow lab partners weren't present yet, so I got to enjoy a few minutes of peace before the gawking set in. Leaning my elbows against its surface, I slid my fingers through my not so neat hair; my glasses shifted on my face as I sighed heavily.

Lunch period was two more classes away. Only ninety minutes left to bite my fingers off in anticipation of Mari's reaction to all this.

five

. . .

STUDENTS TRICKLED into the indoor lunchroom. Long, generic grey tables lined up row after row, with warm bodies on their benches. Some sat in small groups, some in pairs, some alone. Lunchroom etiquette was always kind of awkward. Not everyone ate during the same period, so if all your friends were in a different period, it left you to fend for yourself.

I took a seat in the farthest corner of the cafeteria, hunched over my tray of ham and swiss on a bulky roll, a bag of Lay's potato chips and a can of iced tea. An orange too, but I wasn't much of a fruit eater.

All this shit talk about what happened with Ashley left my stomach in a disagreeable state. The attention to my physical person was uncomfortable in this magnitude. Enough of that balled up into one seven hour school day, took a massive toll on me.

Sliding in from the edge of the bench, Logan came into view with his brown paper lunch bag in hand. He didn't need to say anything, but I knew he would.

"Well," he stated rather casually, "it looks like you have had quite an interesting day."

"Oh, you would know." I might as well blame him for the rumor continuing to circulate. This was exactly something he would do.

"I still can't believe you did that," he chastised, pulling out a foil wrapped sandwich. "Can't believe you're even walking."

"Can we talk about something else, please?" I forced a bite of ham and cheese into my mouth and chewed it up, not even tasting it before swallowing.

"All right." He unfolded the wrapping of his food, placing his hands down flat against the reflective metal of the foil. "Dave asked me to work Saturday night, but I got this thing with my ma."

"Your mom, huh?"

"Seriously dude, it's the 10th anniversary of my aunt dying."

"So you're celebrating?"

"That's messed up, Pete, even for you." He pulled out a can of Coke and popped it open, taking a long drag of caffeinated fuel into his mouth. "My grandma freaks out if she spends the day alone."

"So you're just gonna hang out with her?"

"My ma makes dinner and stuff. She tries to make it as un-awkward as possible. I watch TV all night with my brothers. Some-times my cousins come by, but–"

"All right," I cut him off, "I don't need to hear a play-by-play of how you plan to spend your night. I'll cover you."

I didn't mind. Work was less work and more me reading comic books. Customers came in, sure. Mostly fellow enthusiasts or parents who didn't know what the hell to buy their kid. Simple stuff to deal with and if no Logan or Dave, that meant I'd have the place to myself during downtime.

"Thanks man, I owe you."

He resumed uncovering the contents of his lunch bag when I saw a familiar face. Mari barreled toward our table, her long hair trailing behind her like Superman's cape. She was wearing casual waist high blue jeans and a yellow t-shirt that brought out the tan color of her skin. She was tight-lipped, eyes trained right on me. That face made my stomach somersault a hundred different ways. Now I really didn't want to eat.

Logan turned as she sat down a few feet from him. "Hey, Mari."

"Hey," I squeaked out, without sounding like I was about to be vilified. Tapping her pink painted nails against the linoleum tabletop, she leaned to one side.

"Pete, what the hell am I hearing about you?"

"I don't know." I shrugged. "What are you hearing about me?"

"That you almost got your ass handed to you by Westley De La Cruz… for Ashley?"

Her tone both rose and fell with each word, a sign that her conflicted state had taken over She-Hulk style. She was probably holding back all morning until she could confront me.

I stared at my broken reflection in the leftover foil from Logan's sandwich, only making out my dark-framed glasses and a few shreds of dirty blonde hair. "He was being an asshole. I couldn't just walk away."

Her threaded brows pressed against her eyelids. "And you couldn't tell me this? Why?"

Logan raised his hands. "Give the guy a break."

She eyed Logan with a vicious stare for a quick second before coming back to me. "You told him, didn't you?"

There wasn't a good excuse why I didn't report to her first. It wasn't like I told Logan on purpose. Ashley came to the store, and therefore, the news came with her. Breathing out to relieve the tightness in my chest, I rubbed my forehead, thinking this was worse when compared to standing up to Westley. "How did anyone even hear about this?"

Mari eyed Logan with an expected scowl. "Why not ask your supposed best friend over here?"

"Fuck," I slammed my hands down, "Logan, you said you would keep your mouth shut!"

Raising his hands in protest, Logan swallowed his mouthful of food. "I only told Chris! And… maybe Dante."

"Dante? Why would you tell him? He's ten times worse than you with shit like this!"

"You can tell him, but you can't tell me?" Mari raised an eyebrow to me, her fingertips still tap-tap-tapping in unwinding annoyance.

I looked up at the generic white paneled ceiling before coming back down. "Because I knew you'd freak out, like you're doing now."

"The only reason I'm pissed is because… never mind. I should *not* have to explain myself." Taking in a long, full breath, Mari settled down on the bench. Closing her eyes, she brought her arms in against her chest. "When did you decide not to trust me with stuff like this? I wouldn't have been mad at you, but you kept it from me and now I'm hearing it from everyone else."

Her brown eyes darted over mine, anticipating an answer. There was no answer. I was scared, more scared than when I stepped into this situation. Things with Mari were getting tossed around so much. I had to protect whatever wasn't broken already.

"Can we talk about this later?"

Her lips flattened as leaned against the table and pushed up to stand. "Fine."

She walked away in a huff. All my doing, of course. I didn't even bother to watch her go. I was so tired of making things ten times worse. Go me. Only three more hours of school, thank fucking god.

Logan blew out a long-winded whistle, shaking his head. "Wow, she's pissed."

Glaring at him, I couldn't be too angry. Partially, it was my fault for thinking he could keep a secret, a mistake I will never make again. Logan watched me, his mouth twisting into a knot.

"I'm sorry, Pete. Like, legit sorry."

"Dude," I exhaled, "now you really owe me."

six

. . .

I WAS like a wounded soldier the entire rest of my day after talking to Mari. Dragging along, waiting for the opportunity to breathe and throw all my gear off my back. On the steps of the main entrance to this metropolis of puberty-stricken teens, I sat alone with my head down and my arms hanging between my knees. Despite my buds radiating the epic ballad of "Bohemian Rhapsody" into my eardrums, they failed to blast away the events of the day. I was glad it was over for now. Tomorrow would be some of the same shit. People whispering and staring at me with their own ideas of what a guy like me is up to, associating myself with a girl like Ashley.

At this point, I kind of wished I'd never done it. Was that bad? Wishing I hadn't helped someone after the fact? It was probably normal. I couldn't be the only person where something like this had happened. The Native Americans helped the Pilgrims, and they got shit for it, right? That was an extreme case but the same principle applies.

I watched a few cars drive up to collect people off the stairs. Mostly parents, some friends grabbing friends. This was the general pickup spot for those who didn't take the bus. I usually just walked by myself. I didn't live too far from school and I hated taking the bus, but my sister Kimberly was grabbing me today. No particular reason, just because she felt like it, or demanded it.

A lackluster horn sounded a few cars down the line. Popping my head up, I strained my neck to see if it was her. The car was nice, clean with well-polished rims, a pulse of deep beats radiating from its black painted exterior. Its body hung low, and the muffler rumbled, ready to take off like a pod racer. I couldn't tell you what make or model the car was because there was no hood ornament, which meant it was probably not legal.

Tires screeched as it peeled from the line, obviously in too much of a rush to wait for innocent bystanders to enter their parental taxis. Tinted windows shot past the steps before coming to a screeching halt right behind Mr. Tanny, the not so tall but definitely buff Junior English teacher directing traffic. He raised his hands in protest, shaking his head. "What's the rush, buddy?"

The driver of the car didn't come out, but someone walked up to the ebony beacon that everyone was now gawking at. With a bounce in her step, Ashley tossed her hair from her face, clutching her books to her chest. She had on a plain blue hoodie with straight cut jeans and bright red Converse sneakers. No one wears red sneakers and doesn't expect to draw attention to themselves.

She turned to Mr. Tanny, shifting her hand to one side. "Sorry, Mr. Tanny."

Not bothering to wait around, she opened the door and hopped in the car. I could only assume that the person driving the car was Wes, so I guess their little scrap didn't survive the rest of the weekend. Yet another sign that it probably didn't matter that I did what I did, at least to Wes. Settling back on my step, I watched as Mr. Tanny reluctantly waved the car down the line to exit the parking lot.

The constant thought of her brought the memory of her scent back to the forefront, that fresh spearmint aroma, like a piece of gum that sends shock-waves to your head every time you bite down into it. Refreshing and not at all brutal. I never noticed how much I liked that smell before.

More cars rolled up, and I recognized the silver two-door chariot of my sisters. I threw my bag on my shoulders and walked down the steps. Opening the door, Kimberly looked at me with her dark round sunglasses on, her brown hair kind of meshed up in a swirl bun.

"Hey, short stack," she said as I took a seat and shut the door.

"Why do you still call me that? I'm taller than you."

"Because it bothers the shit out of you." I turned to look at her smirking face, raising an eyebrow.

We followed the line of cars out of the parking lot and made a left onto the main road. Shoving my bag to the floor, I leaned against the window, the car's natural vibrations ringing in my ears.

"What's up?" she asked.

"Oh the usual," I moaned, "being poked and prodded and examined."

"Since when are you the poetic type?"

"Since today."

Leaning toward me with her eyes still on the road, her forehead wrinkled up behind her sunglasses. "Any reason?"

She seemed keen to dig into my words a little deeper, but I should have just kept my mouth shut. I really didn't feel like talking about it anymore. "High school stuff..."

"That good, huh?" Kimberly settled back behind the wheel and we drove on toward home.

The traffic was mild, but the start of rush hour was slowly trickling into the yellow-lined streets. Resuming my vigil at the window, I stared at the streaks of paint separating the lanes on the black road. When I was a kid–well I guess I still am but- I used to pretend I was slowly being launched into space, the rapidly passing lines a sign that I was about to crack through the Earth's atmosphere, to enter the vastness of the universe and beyond. It made long car rides more bearable.

"I don't mean to put another damper on your day," Kimberly's words broke my concentration, "but mom asked me to talk to you about college."

A low, unenthusiastic groan escaped me as I rolled against the headrest. "Of course she did."

"She's got that paper-clipped pile of applications sitting on the kitchen table waiting for you to put a pen to." She glanced at me. "I don't know why you don't tell her you don't want to go."

"It's not that I don't want to go…"

"Then what is it?"

I couldn't think of a lie, not that it would work.

"Look, I can't tell them for you. Speak up for yourself. They will not hate you. They'll get over it. It's your life, not theirs."

Parents… the bane of every teenager's existence. I couldn't complain, they weren't nuts or abusive or anything like that. Our dad worked for the post office, been a mail carrier since he was 18 years old. Our mom, she had held several odd jobs over the years, currently she worked as a receptionist at a dentist's office. Just average American parents working average American jobs. Both hard workers, my dad especially, he grew up pretty poor, so being able to provide for his family was super important to him. My mom was the free spirit, went to college but never settled on one career for very long.

"Home sweet home." Kim pulled into the driveway.

Dad had his Jeep parked out front. It was an average street lined with cars along the curb, making the street even narrower and impossible for anything to pass through. Our house was a generic blue with a gray slated roof and matching shutters. Large green bushes sat under the windows in the front, framing a sand colored stone path leading up to the white painted door. Our garage was a replica of the house in color and was seldom used to store cars. Mostly storage for lawn stuff, bikes, workout gear, and my dad's workbench where he liked to fix everything before calling a professional to fix it for real.

Kimberly turned the key to shut off her car, leaning back in the driver's seat. "Look, glance at the applications so mom thinks I convinced you to apply if you still wanna jerk them around."

"I'm not jerking them around–"

"It sure seems like you are."

Grabbing my bag from the floor, I moved to open the door. "Why do you care so much, anyway?"

"Because it's my job to make sure you don't do anything stupid."

"So going to college is stupid?"

"For you, yes."

"You're going to college–"

"Because I'm an overachiever and always need something to

occupy my brain. You know I can't sit still for shit." She unbuckled her seatbelt. "You don't know what the hell you want. Tons of idiots go to college because it's what you're '*supposed*' to do. It's a waste of your time and money if you have no fucking clue what the hell you want."

"Does anyone really know what they want out of high school?"

"An idea would be nice…"

"Seriously, Kim, just stay out of it!"

Pushing against the seat, I stared up at the unappealing stains littering the ceiling. She was just telling me like it was. I get it, but I couldn't today. No more added bullshit after the day I escaped from. "Sorry… I just… can we not talk about this right now?"

"Fine." Kim popped the door handle and pushed it open, letting one leg out of the car. "Don't drag it out. Trust your gut."

"Right, got it."

"I'm being serious."

"So am I… kind of."

She shook her head. "That's the problem with you, Pete, you take nothing seriously."

I opened my door and stepped out. "Maybe it's time we talk about what you don't take seriously…"

Kimberly gave me that Kubrick *A Clockwork Orange* stare. "Don't turn this around on me."

"Why not? Don't I get to poke at your life for a change?" Closing the door, I waited for her to walk around the car.

"Not without permission."

"Why do I need permission?"

Kimberly smirked, unzipping her dark vegan jacket to tie around her waist. "Because I'm your sister, number one. And number two, you're terrible at reading anyone, especially girls. So even if you tried, you'd fail miserably and end up with a bowl full of lies."

Slinging my backpack onto my shoulder, I looked down at our still yellowish front lawn as we made our way to the house. Number two was so undeniably true, it hurt. If I could read girls at all, I'd know that not telling Mari about what happened was a bad idea. I'd know why the hell Ashley sprung up on me during work hours. And why I couldn't get her eyebrow-raised smirk out of my head.

seven

. . .

THURSDAY. It's been a weird couple of days. People were still talking here and there, but mostly my heroics were forgotten. I wasn't getting any more long-winded stares or head turns as I walked down the halls of the school. Sure, there were still a few gossipers talking about it behind my back but, as long as they were not making it obvious, I really didn't care. Mari wasn't evilly eyeing me anymore, and that was all that mattered to me.

I sat outside the band room with my knees up to my chest, using my legs as a podium to hold up the most recent issue of Your Friendly Neighborhood Spiderman to my scanning eyes. Many people will argue forever who the best superhero was, but Peter Parker is definitely one of my top three. It was not because we shared the same name, although that was a bonus. He was just a kid like any other when his universe turned upside down. A kid trying to navigate through his awkward teen years.... with superpowers. I mean, that sounded like puberty in a nutshell, only I couldn't climb up walls with my fingertips and web sling.

Keeping my nose to the printed pages, I minded my business, and students walked by every now and again. It was well after school hours, but I always waited for Mari while she was in jazz band practice. Rehearsals always lasted at least two hours. Mr. Cello was a funny guy, but when it came to music, he was a stickler for perfection. That's why the band always sounded so good.

As much as I enjoyed listening to them practice the same set of music repeatedly, it wasn't great for comic book reading. So, I had my buds on, streaming some tunes into my eardrums. The Midnight has been constantly on repeat lately. They were one of those bands that didn't have a terrible song in their arsenal.

"Hey."

Jerking my head up from panel surfing Spiderman kicking Doc Oc's ass, I dropped my comic into my lap. There was Ashley, her hair in its usual kinky state surrounding her smooth angular face, her hands smashed between her knees like a sandwich. Her friend Amber was standing behind her, arms folded and legs bouncing in her white sneakers in anticipation. She was wearing her black and orange cheerleading uniform, the words Hicksville Comets strewn across the front and her dark hair done up in a braid. The French kind. Wherever Ashley was, Amber was never too far behind.

"Uh, hi," I said, rather unamused by the sudden interruption.

"What's up?" Ashley pulled herself up a bit, innocent curiosity seeping through every word.

I shrugged. "Nothing really. Just… waiting for Mari."

"She your girlfriend?"

My eyes squinted behind my glasses. What was she getting at with this line of questioning? She seemed genuinely interested in knowing more about me. I didn't want to know the reason. I just wanted this conversation to be over as quickly as possible. It wouldn't go over well if Mari saw her talking to me. I wanted nothing to do with Ashley. But it seemed Ashley wanted something to do with me.

"Yeah," I answered simply.

"And how's that working out for you?"

Hanging my arms over my knees, I looked from Amber's unreadable expression back to Ashley, one eyebrow raised and a slight curve in the corner of her mouth.

"How is that any of your business?" I asked.

"You walked into my business so…"

Amber stepped forward and tugged at Ashley's jeans jacket. "Come on, Ash, let's go."

"Yeah, that's probably a good idea," I flipped the page of my comic, eyeing them uncomfortably.

With a dual brow raise this time, Ashley backed off. "All right. See you around, lover boy."

She turned on her heels and they walked down the hall. Leaning back against the wall, I watched them until they were out of sight.

This would never go away. She would never go away. This shouldn't happen to someone who tried to do the right thing. I wasn't expecting people to hoist me up in the air and throw me a goddamn ticket parade in Times Square, but dammit, I'm done with the reminder. As soon as I thought it was over, it came right back. No more heroic acts from me, at least not until I moved to some place where no one knew me.

The clock across from me, mounted on the plain school wall, landed at five o'clock. I pulled off my ear buds, already hearing the seats shifting and cases being slammed shut as the band was closing another successful practice. Shoving my comic behind my skateboard in my backpack, I stood as people trickled out of the room.

Mari came out, wielding her large black saxophone case while trying to pull her pink JanSport backpack up on her shoulders. I slipped my fingers through the case handle, crossing her own. "Let me get that."

She let me take it for her. "Thanks." She got her backpack through both arms and sighed as she held onto the straps. "You were waiting this whole time?"

"Yeah, don't I always?"

"Did you listen in at all?"

I shook my head. "Nah, I had comics and my tunes to entertain me."

She sighed, almost disappointed. "Listening to anything good?"

"Been having The Midnight on repeat lately."

"Oh, yeah." Her eyes lit up a bit. "I remember you turned me on to that one song of theirs. It had that amazing sax solo."

"A lot of their songs have that."

We continued down the hall, walking together just a centimeter apart. Mari kept looking at me, her mouth upturned as if trying to read something that wasn't there. "I thought you'd be at baseball tryouts."

"Oh, that." Folding my lips between my teeth, I ran my tongue across their chapped surface. "I don't know if I'm going to play this year."

"Why? You're a natural, Pete. Don't you like playing anymore?"

"I do, it's just… I don't know. I'm not feeling it like I used to."

She shrugged. "They'd be less of a team without you."

A small lighthearted breath escaped me. "Are you trying to make me feel guilty or something?"

"Is it working?"

She nudged me down the hall playfully as we rounded the corner toward the main lobby. "Come on, Pete. It's the last time you'd get to play with these guys. I know how much the team means to you and Chris… what would he do without you to hold him together out there?"

"He is rather pathetic."

"See? You already know you should. I'm sure they'd still let you tryout, even though you missed the first day. I mean, you shouldn't even have to try out at this point. Just walk in and they'll throw you a uniform."

"You really think I'm that good, huh?"

"I know you're that good," she said with that amazing smile of hers.

Damn, she always knew how to talk me up on things, that or I was easily manipulated. Coming in closer, she leaned against my shoulder as we walked out of one of the many entrances to the school and down the dozen steps to the parking lot.

"I'm sorry I've been such a bitch to you about the whole Ashley thing."

"Don't worry about it." I shrugged.

"You did the right thing. I get why you didn't tell me."

"And I get why you were upset. I wasn't trying to be an asshole to you."

"I know."

We walked past a few empty spots and parked cars before reaching the line of buses waiting to make the last round of pick-ups for the night. Switching the sax to my outside hand, I wrapped my arm around Mari's shoulders, taking in the smell of her long dark hair, that slight hint of coconut still lingering in every strand. She always smelled so good, there was never a time her scent didn't captivate me.

We got to her bus, and she turned to face me. "Thanks for waiting for me."

Slipping her sax onto the first step of the bus, I smiled. "Yeah, of course."

She grabbed it, holding on to the first seat of the bus. "So, are you trying out or not?"

I shrugged. "I don't know, maybe."

"This can be a big deal for you, like a big scholarship."

"I don't know if I want that."

"Don't you think it's time you figured out what you want? School is over in less than four months, Pete."

As she moved further up the bus, I stepped forward and grabbed her by the wrist. "Hey," I coaxed, "don't I get a little something?"

"Only if you promise to try out."

That sly, almost seductive gleam in her eyes was such a weakness for me. Taking a deep breath, I huffed slowly, letting the air seep out from between my lips like a deflating beach ball. "All right. You talked me into it."

She leaned down and kissed me softly on the lips. "Wise decision."

Slipping her hand out of my grasp, she backed away onto the bus. "See you tomorrow."

"Yeah," I said. "See ya."

She disappeared into the bowels of pleather benches as I stepped back onto the sidewalk. I pulled my skateboard free from my bag, threw it to the concrete, and hopped on.

Things with Mari were officially smoothed over. I couldn't think of a better way to end the day. These kinds of days seemed to be happening more and more often. It was probably normal after a two year relationship to be hitting so many speed bumps. This last one though, was one of the worst. I'd make it a point not to have another like it anytime soon.

Kicking my feet, I steadily dragged the wheels as I pushed forward to gain momentum. I rocked from side to side, avoiding bystanders with ease. As I reached the edge of the school grounds, I turned to my left down the not so busy road of streetlights and dimly lit overhangs of lazy store fronts.

I pulled out my buds again and stuffed them into my ears, pressing the play button on my phone screen to resume my musical vigil. Continuing my kick on The Midnight, "Dream Away" pulsed against my drums and sent my mind into a proverbial chill state. As the lyrics wove a story in my mind, I couldn't help but think of Ashley. That half hook smirk of her's and cocked eyebrow. It was adorable, in a way. Adorable and dangerous at the same time.

eight

· · ·

I WELCOMED the call of employee routine. Weekends at Grasshoppers were always a little busier, and Saturday nights, we ran Magic card tournaments in the small back room for the card gamer nerds of the world. I didn't have the patience to learn it, but I still had to run the tournaments at the store. I had some basic knowledge of how it worked.

Tonight's friendly competition was winding down and the reigning champion, an obscurity shaped fellow named Bruce, had won the night yet again. Bruce was sort of that typical looking obsessive tabletop gamer. He wore plain colored shirts that always looked like he just pulled them out of a pile off his floor. His hair was uncombed, and he wasn't slim, to put it politely. He smelled like Campbell's Soup and had a terrible attempt at facial hair growing on his piggy pimpled face. I wasn't even sure how old he was. My guess was early twenties, maybe forties.

"Another victory under your belt?" I asked, as he lumbered past me at the counter.

"Too easy," he said, rubbing his nose across his arm. "When are you going to find me some actual competition?"

"I'll put out the word online. The bat signal doesn't seem to be working again."

He laughed at that last one. The only thing Bruce had going for him was that he had the same first name as Batman. And when I say the only thing I mean… the only thing.

"Till next week, my good man," he said with a bow of his head.

I followed not too close behind as I didn't want to inhale too much of the soup smell. He was the last of the bodies to vacate the shop, so I quickly swiped the sign from open to close. I only had a few things to do before I could leave. With the drawer counted, I was ready to put it in the safe. All I had to do was grab a spray bottle and wipe down the tables and chairs of the game room.

Slipping on my buds, I pumped some tunes into my ears as I grabbed the non-labeled spray bottle and some paper towels. I wasn't in the mood for anything in particular, so I pressed the shuffle button on my music player and let it choose for me. The sounds of Joy Division's solemn, disjointed pipes leaked in with "Shadowplay". A good end to a night of slaving over colored paper magazines and loud, belligerent voices arguing over if they could stun or had to wait for the next turn. I got through the game room pretty quickly, spraying down the surfaces of everything skin could touch. The chairs had cheap plastic material over them, so I didn't have to scrub any unwanted stains or smells from them too harshly.

After my cleaning tasks were done, I popped open the safe under the counter, slid in my money tray, and shut the door. I was ready to call it a night. Adjusting a few more things here and there, I grabbed my gray sweat jacket and pulled on my red beanie. I took my deck out of my bag, keeping it tucked under my arm as I opened the front door. Taking a last scan of the store, I shut off the lights and stepped outside. The door had a double lock from the outside, fingerprint style. Dave was too cheap to buy a security system, but not too busy to buy a fingerprint lock. I didn't see how that would deter anyone from busting open a window and ransacking the joint, but whatever. To each their own.

Pressing my finger to the door, I waited for the Trekky green light beep, telling me it activated the lock. One more turn of the key and a quick pull on the handle, I was ready to skate my way home to spend the rest of my evening sitting in front of my TV for some co-op Smash Bros. I pulled down my beanie to combat the chill rushing to my face. It was one of those post winter nights, and this one was Mr. Freeze level cold.

Just as I was about to throw my skateboard down onto the sidewalk, a blunt force came down on my shoulder, turning me around to come face to face with the angry curled mug of Wes. His jaw jutted forward with tension as he clenched his teeth, hair pushed back slick and dark like a greaser from The Outsiders. His thick eyebrows pulled down over his trigger-ready eyes.

"I'm talking to you, punk!"

Pulling my buds from my ears, I took an alarming step back. "What? I didn't know you said any–"

"Don't fucking lie to me, you little shit."

Well, this was turning out to be a pleasant, spur-of-the-moment interaction. Wes took a step in my direction, which I matched with a step away from his direction.

"Don't think I haven't been keeping my eye on you," he warned.

"Look, I–"

Rushing forward, he pinned me against the brick wall of the shop, grabbing me by my jacket, breathing his gross smoker's breath all over my glasses.

"You think I would forget what you did? Stepping into my business? Getting between me and my girl, huh?"

His face came closer to mine. I couldn't see through the fog of my glasses, and it erased any words that remotely resembled the English language from my memory.

"You better not even look at her, you got that? Not one fucking look! Or I'll smash your skull in."

Faster than my shocked mind could react, he grabbed my skateboard from under my arm, swinging it right at my head. My flight response was still working, thank god, and I ducked out of the way as my deck smashed against the side of the building. He pulled away and, with my board still in hand, wrecked it against a small but impressively durable tree standing across from us. I winced as the front truck broke free from the deck, now bent and split across the tail-end of the board.

Wes threw the remaining parts of my board at me, which I barely caught. Well, I caught part of it, anyway. Glancing down at what he left of my mode of transportation and recreational joy, I scanned every bruise and splinter now embedded across its body. This was one of the first boards I ever got, and now it was totaled. Unimaginably totaled.

Wes grabbed me by my jacket again, pulling right up to his scowling face. "I'll be watching you. Don't fucking cross me again, understand?"

Nodding my head like a psychopath, he stormed off under the streetlights, his fists jammed in his pockets. I stood there, still in a state of proverbial shock at what the last sixty seconds of my life just were. I took a deep, nervous breath.

"Holy shit…"

I leaned back on the headrest of Chris' backseat, staring at the water-stained ceiling. Logan was up front in the passenger seat, sticking his feet out the window for anyone interested in taking a whiff of his walkers as they drove by.

It was Sunday. The news of Wes almost ending my life got as far as Chris and Logan. And I planned to keep it that way. The dismal body of my dismembered board lay in my lap as we embarked to Bleacher Street Skate, me and Logan's favorite skateboard shop. I hoped it was salvage-able and, if not, leave with a new board and whatever dignity I had left.

"Well, Pete," I heard Chris say, "you've gotten your first little taste of the shit you've willingly stepped in."

"Thanks for reminding me."

Drawing my gaze down toward the worn out seat beside me, I stared at the broken pieces of my skateboard. This is evidence that not all good deeds avoid punishment.

Chris shook his head. "You're lucky he didn't lay you out. You're lucky it was just your skateboard!"

I held up my never-to-ride-again deck, waving it in the rearview mirror with a maddening stare. "You call this luck?"

Wes was not fucking around. That was blatantly clear. Sinking back down in my seat, I leaked my exhale through the gaps of my teeth, that big tyrant's words on repeat in my head.

I chewed on my bottom lip, closing my eyes. Wes acted like I was intentionally seeking Ashley out, but she was the one instigating it. All of it. Maybe I was seeing her more often than I ever cared to notice, but that was only because of what had happened. Your brain does that. Now I was programmed to pick her out of a crowd, and she missile targeted me every time.

"So," Logan said, "you're going to tell Mari, right?"

"Are you insane?" I said.

"I think you should tell her," Chris added. "This is getting out of hand."

"And how would telling her make it seem less out of hand?"

"Yeah." Logan sighed. "It'll make it worse."

Chris glanced back at me. "You promised her you wouldn't keep shit from her, and here you are, keeping shit from her."

I looked out the window as we came to a stoplight. "I'm treading on thin ice as it is."

"All the more reason to tell her. You want to make it worse for yourself?"

"Look, it's none of your business," Logan said.

"He's our friend, man." Chris' attention returned to the road as the light turned green. "Look. Pete, I'm just trying to help you out."

"I know, I know." I leaned forward onto my knees. "And you're right, I should tell her."

Thinking about telling Mari just reminded me of how different things were between us. When we first started dating, everything was light and carefree. But when senior year hit, everything shifted. Now, it was serious. Mari kept everything grounded, structured even. Did this happen to everyone who was ready to become an adult? If so, I was far, far away from being ready. I didn't want high school to end, not like she did.

Logan turned in his seat, taking his feet out of the window. "Things aren't the same with her, are they?"

"Is it that obvious?" I rolled my head back against the headrest, forcing the air from my lungs.

"Then tell her or it's going to get worse." Chis added as he looked down the cross street, "What the fuck street is this place on again?"

"Bleacher," Logan answered, "the best skate shop on the island."

I sat in silence, staring at the frequently vacuumed floor, listening to the sounds of cars and directional blinkers. Mari and me. It felt like our relationship was slipping through my fingers. All the pressures of senior year. Maybe it was that. She had to be feeling it from her parents like I was, but she seemed to know what she wanted. Like she had everything planned out perfectly. I didn't. I had no direction. Maybe that was why everything felt so messy.

"Thanks for taking me out here," I uttered.

"No problem," Chris replied. "You know we got your back."

nine

. . .

"HOW MANY SETS ARE THERE?"

Rina hung over the bannister. It was toward the end of the school day, and Chris' last track meet of the season was about to start. They packed the bleachers with parents, siblings, and students as they were getting ready to watch. The weather had held up, but the chill that followed the final days of winter still creeped on. The bleachers weren't what I'd call luxury seating arrangements, and the cold settled deep within the bones of the metal.

Looking left of the rubber squared track, Chris and the other runners stretched and readied themselves for the next race. A lot of them wore the school colors they represented; Mineola, Levittown, and Westbury, to name a few. Winter track gear was more snug than the usual tank and shorts. Tight running pants and long sleeve athletic wear kept the sweat in and the adrenaline pumping as they placed themselves into position on the line. Chris was on the fifth line, an orange sweatband proudly displaying the "H" of Hicksville.

"It's not tennis, Rina," Mari grinned. "It's just called a race or… whatever." Rina turned and raised an eyebrow, a clamped grin plastered across her small round face.

"Well, you learn something new every day." She scooted back next to Mari, getting really close as she shoved her hands in her jacket pockets and hunkered down beside her to collect any possible body heat. I sat on Mari's other side, her arm tightly hooked into mine.

The starting gun shot into the air as runners sprang into action, scrambling for that golden mushroom… I mean, metal or whatever, they gave the winners. The runners were all a blur as they ran toward the finish line. Chris was in the lead, but another was closing in. Mari slipped out of my arm as I strained to see who crossed first.

"Smash'em up, Chris!" I shouted as clapping and cheers escalated from the finish. From what it looked like, East Meadow was the clear victor. But I call bullshit. They just didn't call it from the right angle. Settling back down, Mari shook her head at me as the next set of runners was getting into position.

"I don't think that helped," she said as she laced her arm back through mine.

"Doesn't make it any less necessary," I replied.

Her lips curled as she bared her teeth with an annoyed smugness too cute to be considered a scold. She drew her head down on my shoulder briefly, pushing against me.

"You're a lost cause."

Rina turned to us. "So, are you trying out for baseball, Pete? I heard Mari talked you into it."

"She could talk me into an oven."

"So I take it that's a yes."

"He should." Mari looked at her. "He's the best they've got besides Chris."

"I think it's great you're sticking it out, Pete. That's something you might regret later on."

I shrugged. "I don't think I'd regret it, but I'll do it for the team."

"Regardless," Mari turned back to me, "it's a chance at a scholarship. That's huge!"

"Who says I want it?"

Mari's eyes twisted with intensity. "It'd be stupid not to take it. A free pass for four years of college? There are so many others who'd kill for it."

"Well, where's the line start?"

A light chuckle escaped Rina's lips from behind her pink gloved hands.

"God, don't you take anything seriously?" Mari asked, pulling away from me.

"Sure, I just don't want a baseball scholarship."

"Whatever, Pete." She folded her arms over her chest as another shot went off to start the second race. We watched the runners zoom past, but we were far less interested. Chris would run again in a few.

"Where's Logan?" Rina asked. "Shouldn't he be here by now?"

"You'd think that, but this is Logan we're talking about," I added as the runners zoomed past us. I stood to get a better look as they were nearing the finish line.

Crossing her legs, Mari adjusted her position. "He's another one. Everything is a free ride to him." She looked at me. "No wonder you two get along so well."

"Hey, I am far more serious than Logan." I sat back down. "Not to shit on him or anything."

"He just has a different outlook on life," Rina said. "Some people are just like that."

"Where does he hope to end up, does he ever think of that?" Mari raised a brow at me.

I expelled a long, drawn out breath. "Probably not, but I know he wants to go pro with skateboarding. He had that guy reach out to him and everything for that new training school in California."

"Like I said," she rolled her eyes back out toward the track, "a match made in heaven."

I settled my focus back onto the field. She was in rare form today, barking more demands than usual. Mari had always been headstrong and extremely hardworking, and I admired that about her. It was one of the things that first attracted me to her. But seriously, she had to pump the breaks every once in a while. Life wasn't always about where you were going to end up. If we always focused on the future, we'd all be dead before we hit thirty years old. Talk about burnout. I'd much rather be indecisive than bat shit focused.

"Aww, look at the cute little couple," a familiar female voice rang.

We looked as Ashley and Amber came up the stairs with a few

stragglers behind them. I guess seeing us was far too tempting to ignore. Lucky for me. They passed by us slowly. I didn't care about what she said, however Mari eyeballed her like she was about to jump down Ashley's throat.

They passed without incident, to my utter relief, and we watched them walk up the steps toward the top of the bleachers.

"What is with her?" Mari looked away with a sigh.

Ashley sat down, resting her feet on the empty bench in front of her. She wore another pair of converse, this time purple. I wondered how many pairs she had. She started laughing about something, falling into Amber who just rolled her eyes while trying to hide a smirk. Leaning her head back for a moment, her eyes found mine.

I acted like anyone who just got caught staring would. Like I was looking at something else. Turning slightly to the right, I saw an older couple attempting to throw popcorn in each other's mouth.

"Enjoying the view?"

I whipped my head around, Mari eying me closely.

"What?" I pointed behind me with my thumb. "Popcorn couple?"

"No." she gestured up toward Ashley with a nod. "Her."

"Oh," I shrugged, "I like her shoes."

"And that's all?"

"Yeah. That's all."

I looked back out toward the track. Chris was lining back up at the starting line. Pressing off my hands, I raised myself from the bleachers to assess his competition. I could feel Mari's eyes boring into me the entire time, like she had heat-vision or something with equal intensity.

Turning around, I squinted behind my glasses. "Do I have a kick me sign on my back or something?"

"There's something you're not telling me," she spoke heavily, "and it revolves around Ashley, doesn't it?"

Crap. I slowly brought myself back onto the bench. There was no way I could keep myself from telling her what happened now, but my insecure self would try to skirt around it for a little longer.

"What makes you say that?"

"You're acting all jittery, like you can't sit still. That means you're hiding something."

"Is that what that means?"

Mari slapped me on the arm as I came down to sit. "Pete, are you serious right now?"

With a mouthful of hot air, I got a glance at Rina, who looked at me with an uncertainty, her mouth down-turned. My nerves were creeping in on me, crawling along the lining of my stomach like hungry ants. Chris was right. I should have told her because this felt like it was going to be a lot worse.

Looking back at Mari, I sat up as straight as my body would allow. "Wes smashed my skateboard."

Mari blinked with morose surprise running behind her eyes.

"That's horrible!" Rina brought her hand to her chin.

"When did this happen?" Mari questioned forcibly.

"After work last weekend." I tried to speak as calmly as possible. "He was waiting for me outside."

"He knows where you work?" Rina asked. "Did he try to hurt you?"

I quickly adjusted my glasses. "Does attempting to take my head off with my skateboard count?"

"Why would he do that?"

"I don't know." I shrugged. "He was pissed about what I did, I guess. He doesn't want me around Ashley."

"And have you been?" Mari's face was rigid. I don't think she blinked since before I started telling her what happened.

"No, not on purpose."

"Thank god you weren't hurt." Rina sighed, shaking out her hands. "What a jerk that guy is."

I relaxed a little, but Mari wouldn't stop drilling me with her eyes. There was nothing left to say. Moving my hand to her, I tried to rest it in her lap.

"I'm sorry I didn't tell you. I swear that's all that happened."

"That's all, huh?" Pulling away from me, she stood abruptly, her fists balled at her sides. "You still don't get it do you?"

"Mari, are you okay?" Rina rose next to her, placing a hand on her shoulder.

"I need a minute."

She walked off to the left, toward the stairs leading under the bleachers. Standing up, I thought of reaching for her but stopped myself. I dragged out an endless sigh.

"Hey." Logan's voice sounded in front of me. "I saw Mari, she looked pissed."

"Yeah."

"Go talk to her." Rina pulled my arm. "We'll be here."

Bringing my head down, my eyes rolled up to the top of the bleachers. Ashley was looking at me, completely detached from the conversation carried on by her pack of friends.

"Pete, go!"

Rina pulled me forward, and I launched my feet in the direction where Mari disappeared. The tingling in my stomach turned to a heaviness, causing me to drag my feet along the metal stands.

Holding my breath as we stood under the bleachers, I roughly scrubbed the side of my face with my hand. I had to face what I tried to run away from. The big question was, why did I run?

Mari just stood there, arms folded, eyes focused on me and my inability to do anything right.

"I didn't want you to worry about it," I finally said. "It's not worth the aggravation."

"Telling me is aggravating for you?"

"No, that's not what I meant."

"Then what do you mean, Pete? Because last I checked, I'm still your girlfriend, but you can't trust me?"

"What are you talking about? Of course I trust you."

She shook her head, looking down at her dark blue sneakers. "I don't know why I wasn't the first person you called when this happened." Her gaze came back up to me. "Do Logan and Chris know?"

She stared at me, tapping her fingers against her arm. No matter how I worded the truth, it would sting.

"Yeah, they drove me to get a new board."

"Un-believable."

Okay, she was right. I should have told her sooner, but what could she have done? It wasn't like she could avenge my skateboard or stand up to Wes if he ever showed up again. Or maybe she could. She probably would be more successful at it than me. Regardless, she would take this as an attack no matter what I did.

"I just didn't want you to get involved any more than you already were."

"You think you have to protect me from this Westley and Ashley bullshit? You think I can't handle it?"

"No, that's not it–"

Breathing a cloud of warm carbon breath into my face, Mari gritted her teeth, her dark eyes locking away all the disappointment that was coursing through her veins. "I will be the judge of what I can and can't handle, not you."

Well, if that wasn't a big shot to my already failing ego. She turned away, walking back into the artificial light of the stairs and up into the bleachers. Letting my chin fall to my chest, I stayed hidden beneath the metal cave of horizontal beams and rubber soles. Walking to the far end, I scratched my fingers against the side of my head.

The ants inside my stomach built up so much, they threatened to eject the contents up my throat and out my mouth. I didn't want to move forward, but sure as hell didn't want to go back either. I was stuck in this endless loop of fucking up, and I wasn't sure how to get out of it.

"Wow," Ashley's unwelcomed voice sounded in my ears. She was peeking her head down from the end of bleachers, her hair hanging down like a fancy feather duster from the edges of her hood.

"Go away." I said, turning from her.

"I would," she said as I heard her feet hit the ground behind me, "but sadly, that minor episode of yours was hard to ignore when I heard my name dropped like that."

"So you're eavesdropping on me?"

She swung herself around a pole to get in front of me. "You know, you're just making things worse for yourself."

"Glad you've realized that." I snapped my head around to say something snarky, but opted out of making things worse. "Just… leave me alone. You know nothing about me."

Shrugging, her body shifted to the right, bouncing off her leg for a moment as she folded her arms. "I don't have to know anything about you to see that she's done."

I took a few lengthy strides away from her, closing my eyes to calm myself down. I was ready to punch the next inanimate object I came across, if it wasn't a thick metal pole. Where was my Hulk smashing strength when I needed it? What was with everyone mouthing off? I guess no one kept to themselves anymore.

"Did he really break your skateboard?"

The question stopped me in my rage driven tracks. Looking behind me, she stood patiently, arms crossed, eyebrows flexed in my direction. Her head leaned to her left, like she always seemed to do when she was waiting for something she knew she would get. Goddammit, I never talked to this girl my entire life, and I'm already picking up on the annoying shit that she does.

"It's fine." I breathed as calmly as I could.

"Bastard." She sighed. "I'm sorry he's such an asshole."

"I don't need your apology."

With a smirk, she slowly slid over to me, planting herself to my right. "Well, what do you need?"

With the lights from the bleachers reflecting in her hazel eyes, I couldn't think of what to say. They harbored an odd mix of confidence and curiosity that wildly attracted me. My mouth turned to sand, tiny fragments of shell and rock sticking into my tongue and behind my teeth.

I needed a sign, a slap in the face, anything to shake myself free of all this unharnessed pressure that was bearing down on me. If it wasn't Mari, it was college. If not that, it was baseball or something else. I wanted to figure it out already so I could stop thinking I was making the wrong decisions. Why did everyone seem to have it all figured out and I didn't? It wasn't like I wasn't smart enough, but there was something keeping me from heading in any one direction.

"You should figure that out," she said, her voice shaking me free of my thoughts for a second. Her hand fell on my arm as she backed away to where she dropped in from. "See ya around, Pete."

"You won't," I said.

"Don't worry," she smiled. "I got you."

Whatever that could have meant. Blowing some more hot air into the frosty night, I shook myself back to reality with a sluggish groan. I had to figure stuff out with Mari while avoiding any eye contact or uncomfortable physical interaction with Ashley.

Yeah, piece of cake.

ten

. . .

THAT LITTLE SPAT with Mari moved me to the avoid-at-all-costs level the next few days at school. Nothing was more uncomfortable than having your girlfriend completely ignore you. Couldn't say I wasn't used to it, or at least I never wanted to get used to it. In the past when Mari and I would fight, which was far less than it has been lately, we'd maybe take a day to settle down. Then come right back with apologies and confessions of dip shittery. Couple's fight, it happens, but when they happen more and more, that doubt settles in like a brain slug. The old me would have tried to talk to her way before day two hit. But knowing this was entirely my fault, that my stupidity and inability to not suck could take over yet again, I thought it best just to let it lie.

After school was a little easier to get through than during lunch. I didn't even see her in the cafeteria, which meant she probably ate somewhere far from where I would be. I was glad Mari talked me into going out for baseball again; I needed the physical distraction from all this shit reigning down on me over the last few weeks.

Sitting behind the fence of the well-raked baseball diamond, I re-tied my cleats and rubbed the copper dust off my sweatpants. Chris was next to me, chewing a big wad of Big League with his hand buried inside his glove. It was the last day of tryouts, and if you didn't already quit, the team was pretty much set. Chris and I were in, him taking the captain's spot. A few other regulars also made it, Tom, Dante, and Marcus.

The five of us had made the team every year since we were freshmen. We were the only seniors on for our last remaining year at Hicksville High. The rest were a smorgasbord of a few sophomores, juniors, and one or two freshmen. Most of the newbies wouldn't see base time all season, depending on their skill, but that was where we all started at some point.

"Mari talking to you yet?" Chris asked casually.

I shook my head. "I am on the top of her shit list this week."

"Damn, she must have been really pissed off to give you the silent treatment."

Tom, who was the usual starting pitcher, stood on the mound to wind up his arm. He was tall, taller than me, with shaggy brown hair and an arm that always strikes first and hard mercilessly. He was a guy I would describe as cheeky, always smiling about something.

One of the newer kids was at bat, his dark helmet reflecting against the sun, and feet dug in as he readied himself to swing.

"I told you man," Chris shook his head, "you should have told her."

"Yeah, yeah. I know. Too late to do anything about it now."

"You've been with her this long. You have got to show her respect. She deserves it. Putting up with your bullshit."

"Whose side are you on again?"

With a lightning quick snap, Tom sent the baseball sailing through the air. It was his fastball, one of his most popular pitches to strike out the opponent. The sophomore swung, but way too late. The ball was already deep in the catcher's mitt, practically smoking from impact.

"What's up, ladies." Dante slid in next to Chris, his dark curly hair sticking out from underneath his black and orange baseball cap. He was the type of guy who always had something to say about everything. Call it wit, though I think he was the only one who would call it that. Aside from that aspect of his personality, he was an okay dude. Funny as hell, which came in handy on days like today. He played third basemen or outfielder on the team. I'd never seen someone tag as many players out during a game as him.

Looking out toward the field, he pulled off his cap for a second to run his hands through his hair. "So how's this kid?"

"Pretty good," Chris replied. "He hasn't been able to hit a single one of Tom's fastballs though, few people can."

"Leave it to Tom to give these rookies a hard time." He looked at me. "So how's the whole Ashley thing going for you, Petey boy?"

I cringed. "There is no Ashley thing."

"That's not what I've heard…"

"Come on," Chris interjected, "give it a rest. He's already in the doghouse with Mari about it."

I gave Chris a swift jab to his arm. "What the hell Chris?"

"Geez." Chris pulled his arm back. "Chill out, man."

Another fastball settled in the catcher's glove, with a crash so loud it sounded like someone was swinging Thor's hammer at the ground. It took me out of the conversation for a second, but not long enough for me to be totally unaware of how much my personal life was now public.

"How are you going to get yourself out of this one?" Dante asked.

I cracked my knuckles in my lap. "No clue."

"When's the last time you took her out? Like, on an actual date."

I curled my lips in between my teeth, trying to come up with the most recent date of memory. There was that camping trip we took in October, but that was with a bunch of us, not one on one. The mall a few times… though the mall was not a date. Walking around and hitting up the food court just didn't have the same romantic finesse. There were a few other small things here and there I could think of, but nothing that could qualify as a date.

"I don't know." I shrugged.

"Isn't her birthday coming up soon?" Chris asked.

A part of me wanted them to stop pushing it. The thought of taking Mari out felt more like a death wish than anything that would heal what was broken. Maybe I just needed to sit on it, because it was inching up my throat in suffocating waves.

"Well, there's your answer, my friend." Dante raised his arms in victory. "Take her on a date for her birthday, do something you haven't done in a while… wait, have you done *her* in a while?"

"Oh my god, how old are you?" Chris asked.

"Come on, we're seniors, I think about getting laid, like, a hundred times a day." Dante leaned in on his knees. "You have fucked her at least once, right?"

"Wow, can you shut up, please?" Chris insinuated.

I raised my eyebrows. I wasn't someone who aired out my dirty laundry to just anyone, especially Dante. "I don't see how my sex life is any of your business, dude."

Have Mari and I had sex… well, yeah. A few times. She was my first, and I was hers. I realized it was cliché to think that my first would be my only, but I thought that, at least before this year. Thinking about it now, it had been a few months since I had even seen her in just her underwear.

"Regardless, take her out." Dante shrugged, his hands coming up. "Who knows? It might end with you getting some!"

That would be nice, kind of exciting to think about. But it was short-lived. I didn't think Mari would want to, not with all the shit I'd been pulling lately. And I couldn't if she couldn't.

"Disregarding that last part, I agree with this sexaholic for once." Chris pulled his sleeves up a bit. "Take her out, just the two of you. She'll probably really like it."

Nodding, I looked back toward the field as the sophomore struck out and another was stepping up to the line. It was a good idea. It would show her how sorry I am for screwing up and that I wanted to work on our relationship. Maybe this was what I needed to hear to get my head on straight.

"Yeah," I sat up a little straighter, "I'll do that."

"It's foolproof as long as you don't mess up," Dante added.

A harsh whistle blew, radiating in my ears.

"All right boys, let's call it a day." the coach said, waving his arms. "King, Landon, Goia, grab that stuff behind you and get these boys to the locker room!"

The three of us stood, grabbing the ball bags, baskets and water cooler off of the bleachers. Slinging a bat bag on my shoulder, we started on our trek toward the locker rooms. The other guys grabbed stuff from the field and fell in behind us. Tom and Marcus met up with us in front, each with equipment in hand.

"Some of these new guys need a good oiling up," Marcus said with his deep, monotone voice. He had the deepest voice for a 17-year-old I had ever heard. That made him very popular with the ladies, and I can't blame them. I mean, I would melt if he ever serenaded me with those sweet pipes of his.

"Oh, you'd like to oil them up, wouldn't you?" Dante smiled.

"Sometimes I forget you're here, Dante." Marcus sighed reluctantly.

We got a good chuckle out of that. Taking a step closer to Tom, I adjusted my shoulder strap to keep my bag from slipping. "Good arm today."

"I don't disappoint, even during tryouts," he said.

"Threw some pretty sweet fast ones," Chris added. "As always."

"I think we have a chance at the playoffs this year." Tom shook the excitement from his stride. "I can feel it."

"You say that every year." Marcus switched his glove to his opposite hand. "And it never happens."

"Hey, we made it to the semi's last year," Tom reminded us. "That's got to mean something."

"We got lucky, is what it means," Marcus said.

I put my hand on his shoulder. "Ye of little faith."

"Speaking of luck..."

Dante's finger rose from his side as we reached the last stretch of blacktop before the locker room doors. Leaning against the side of the building with arms folded, that expectant smile on her face, was the bane of the last few weeks of my existence.

"Hey there, boys in uniform."

I hadn't seen Ashley since the track meet. She had on her usual jeans and dark blue sweat jacket with those red sneakers again. A canvas green messenger bag was slung across her chest and headphones draped around her neck. The entire team just stopped at the sight of her, like an anomaly blipping on a radar screen. Shaking off my discomfort, I knew exactly who she was here for.

She bounced over to us, her hands in her pockets with her head tilted to one side, watching me as if I should have known this was going to happen. She stopped in front of me, pulling one hand out to grab mine. Bringing it toward her, she slapped a hundred-dollar bill in my palm, forcing my fingers to grasp it. "For your skateboard."

I shook my head, looking down at my hand, now one hundred dollars richer. "I'm not taking this."

"Then don't," she said as she released me, "but I'm not taking it back." She took several steps back. "Leave it on the ground for all I care."

"Come on…"

"Can't hear you!" She threw on her red Beat headphones and turned away, raising her arm above her head as she waved goodbye in her departure.

I crumbled the money into my fist, feeling the team's collective breathing on my back as they hovered over me like vultures.

Just perfect. One more thing Wes can beat me up for.

eleven

. . .

NOTHING GOT TOO OUT of hand with the money exchange between Ashley and me. Unlike Logan, the team kept it pretty under wraps for my benefit. Not that they hadn't let me forget it during practice. It was more of an inside thing amongst the team, and it stayed that way more or less.

I had told Mari about it when I saw her the next day. If I wanted to break this cycle, I couldn't keep anything from her, not anymore. I cared too much about her to lose her to my shitty ways. She seemed satisfied. Even said it was big of Ashley to give me anything for what Wes did to my board. Afterward, I asked her to meet me at the skatepark where I would be with Logan after school. I hadn't asked her out yet, but I would soon.

On the way, I spotted Amber talking to some other cheerleaders by the entrance of the gym. They were dressed for practice, short gym shorts, school T's and hair in ponytails.

I wanted to let Ashley know I appreciated her gesture of kindness, despite it raising hairs with the team. She didn't have to give me anything to compensate for the mess Wes made of my skateboard. That was really cool of her. As much as I wanted to thank her face to face, I didn't think an upfront approach would work with Wes looming in the shadows.

"Hey, Amber," I said as I came up to her.

All eyes fell on me. Amber's usual accusing stare outweighed some of her amused curiosity. I swear, she never looked happy.

"Yeah?"

"Can I ask you something?"

With a heavy sigh, she looked at her fellow leaders of the cheer variety. "Give us a minute, yeah?"

The other girls made themselves scarce. Falling into the gym, swinging the door closed. Amber looked at me again, arms crossed. "Well?"

"I just wanted you to tell Ashley thanks for–"

"The money?"

My eyes widened a little behind my glasses. She already knew, and why shouldn't she? I was sure Ashley told Amber everything that went on in her life. I thought we would keep this random act of kindness a secret. Not sure why I thought that. Kind of stupid now that I thought about it. "Uh, yeah."

"Why can't you tell her yourself?"

"A wild guess? He's big and breathes fire through his teeth."

"Oh, him." She looked past me, shifting her weight. "I don't like Wes anymore than you do. He's a low-life piece of shit. I've been trying to get Ashley to dump his ass for a year now," she huffed loudly as she folded her arms. "I'm sorry Wes was an asshole to you, but you poking around isn't making it any easier for Ash."

"Trust me, I am not intentionally trying to be in the same vicinity as Ashley for any length of time."

"I know." Her dark ponytail swished from one side to the other as her mouth twisted into an annoyed scowl. "God, I wish she would just shut up about–" She bit her lower lip to stop herself from spilling anything else out. With a quick snap of her neck, she tossed her hair out of her face. "She's been through a lot."

"And Wes is making it easier for her?" I held my breath after I blurted that out. Why should I even care if she was with that prick? It wasn't any of my business, but knowing that she refused to leave a guy who was nothing but a fireball of destruction made me want to protect her. I didn't even know her, and yet I knew if I ever saw him yelling at her like that again, I'd probably do exactly what I had done the first time. Another sign that something was clearly wrong with me.

"You and I both know the answer to that, but Ash can't let go." She took a step back as her dark eyes darted at the gym door, clearly ready to bolt the hell out of my vicinity. "I appreciate what you've done, really I do."

"I wasn't expecting that, but thanks, I guess."

She scoffed. "I'm not a complete bitch, Pete." Turning around, she did a little wave of her fingers, like she was shooing me away. "You can leave now."

I did as I was told and beat it. As I made my way toward the school exit, something she said kept replaying in my mind repeatedly. Ashley wouldn't shut up about something… but what?

My thoughts wrapped around everything that had happened since. A lot of things got stirred up, things I wish I could take back, but there was something that was poking to get my attention. Something that was unexpected. Ashley was at my job. She came up to me in the hall after school. She found me under the bleachers. She planted a Ben Franklin in the palm of my hand.

A bulb went off in my head at this sudden realization that she was actively seeking me out, stepping in to get my undivided attention. I wasn't mad about it. Maybe in the moment, sure, but now… I kind of didn't mind.

✳

"So, things looking up for you two then?" Logan asked as he kicked up on top of the ramp where I was sitting.

Rubbing my hands along the fresh face of my new board, I looked up at him. "Maybe."

"Well about time, I'm tired of seeing her at your throat."

"She's not at my throat."

"Yeah, she's a fucking tiger, man. You are a cub in comparison."

He sighed as he looked out into the watercolor painted sky. The skatepark was part of an even bigger park that was your dictionary definition of what a park was: grass, trees, wide open spaces, baseball field, tennis courts, and even a community swimming pool. There were a few ramps, metal bannisters to grind on, lifts and dips here and there to perform various tricks. Not the biggest place to bring a board, but it was decent for a weekday afternoon.

"Going to break that board in yet?" Logan asked.

The new board I got wasn't anything special. The deck had some swirling colors of black and white with a little crazy looking troll guy on it, mouth open wide to show off three exceedingly large teeth. I never liked the feel of a new board, but they've got to get broken in somehow.

I placed it down to hang over the ramp. Getting my foot positioned on the back, I dropped with considerable ease, letting the wind fold against my face as I sailed to the other side. I grabbed the edge of the ramp as I turned myself around in midair, coming back down on the other side to continue my back and forth pacing on this virgin piece of wood. I didn't plan on doing anything crazy. Doing tricks on a new board is like trying to leap across a tall building with your shoes untied. Not going to happen.

I really just needed to ride this thing every single day to loosen it up with my weight, but hitting some air was nice, too. It was intense for anyone who has never done it before. Once you get past the fear of falling on your ass every five minutes, it's like flying, the closest I will ever get to being Superman.

"Not bad, not bad," I heard Logan say as I made a pass on the other side before falling back down the ramp. A few more reps and I was ready. Just one more run. Coming back down on the concrete surface, my foot came too close to the edge of my board, causing me to break from the deck to use the ramp like a slide.

I lay there, in the middle of the ramp, looking up at the clouds rolling over my head.

"You all right, man?" Logan came sliding down next to me. He gave me his arm, and I took it. He pulled me up, stopping my still rolling skateboard.

"Yeah, I'm good."

We walked off the ramp and made our way to the metal stairs to climb back up.

"Hey, did you hear anything from that California X-Games dude?" I asked.

Logan looked back at me as we made it to the top. "Nah, man, but he said it could be awhile. They're in full construction mode to get everything ready for the summer opening."

I loved skateboarding, but for Logan, it was his life.

"When you hear from him, I know it'll be good news," I reassured him.

"I'll go to California, anyway. With or without a word from him."

Shaking my head, I couldn't help but let out a slight chuckle. "Right, like you could afford it."

"Where there's a will, there is a way, my friend."

We hit the ramp again. I fell four additional times while Logan fell zero.

"When's the last time you rode this one?" he asked.

"It's been a while… like summer?"

"Damn," he said as he met me again where I had fallen, "I guess I just spend too much time here to not know what it's like to totally suck."

I adjusted my glasses. "Laugh it up fuzzball."

He shook his head wildly, raising his arms up in protest to my Star Wars reference. "No, no, you can't pull a Han Solo on me for that."

"I just did."

"What did you do?" We turned our heads as Mari came walking up with her black leather bag hanging over her shoulder, her hair draped over the opposite, hands tucked in the pockets of her waist high jeans that showed off her curves.

"Just you know, pulled a Han."

"Wow, it must have been pretty terrible." She smiled as she stood over us before we both popped to our feet.

"He said I sucked at skateboarding, which makes no sense at all."

"It makes total sense after all the wipeouts you just landed," Logan said.

"Well, I know for a fact you don't suck at skateboarding." Mari raised an eyebrow at him. "So who cares what he thinks?"

Logan held a hand to his heart. "Ouch, way to make my opinion feel appreciated, Mari." Logan walked toward the stairs off the ramp again. "I'll let you two do whatever it is you do. I got a ramp to ride."

We stepped off the concrete ramp and moved a few feet away. "So, how was band practice?"

"The usual." Mari said as we walked toward the skate rail. "I got that solo though."

"Nice! I mean, you're the best they've got, so who else would it go to, right?"

She shrugged. "I guess." Then she smiled at me. Mostly her eyes did, but damn, I couldn't help but get trapped by those eyes of hers. "So, why did you want me to meet you here?"

"Can't I just want you around like, all the time?"

"That would get annoying really fast."

"For you or me?"

"Hmm… good question."

I had to laugh at that. Getting in closer, she grabbed the sleeve of my jacket. "Now, why did you really want me to come here?"

She was enticing, acting like she was actually interested in me, and I liked it. "I heard of a little movie-thon happening relatively soon. Hitchcock related."

"Oh, really?"

"Yeah, really." I took her hand, which was still lingering on my arm. "Want to blow this pop stand and go with me?"

An infectious smile stretched her beautiful, full lips across her face. "I thought you'd never ask."

"All right then. Sounds like a date."

"A date? Haven't had one of those in a while."

"Oh well, it's a good thing I asked you then."

"Yeah, it is."

Coming in close, Mari placed her hand on my chest, leaning up on her tippy toes to plant a slow, timeless kiss on my lips. Like any normal guy, I kept her from stopping, pulling her arm to me as we let our tongues do the talking for us. Man, she tasted so fucking good. The sweetness of her just took over every nerve ending in my body. I missed this. I missed her. Fucking hell, I missed her.

Her pulling away was the worst thing in the entire world, but I let her, still keeping her hand hostage.

"I'd like to have another one of those," I suggested.

"With a cherry on top?"

I raised my eyebrows. "Is that an option?"

"Maybe…"

We kissed again, this time a little more aggressively at how much we were pressing against each other. If we weren't in a public place, I swear there would be clothes flying off in every direction. Wrapping my arms around her waist, I held her there as we kept our mouths on one another. I never wanted to let her go.

"I… I gotta go," she said with a free breath, pushing against my chest.

"Where to?"

"My parents are taking me out for the solo thing. I'd invite you, but my dad hates you."

"Thank you for sparing me."

She smiled, running her finger down my lips. "I'll see you tomorrow?"

"Or… maybe you could come by later?"

She shook her head. "Not on a school night."

"It's never stopped you before."

"I don't think it's a good idea. My dad… you know how he is."

The high I was on from that kiss was slowly deflating, like someone just ripped the Infinity Gauntlet from my arm, taking away all the power and hope I possessed for that brief ten-second period.

"All right, I'll see you tomorrow then."

With a grin, she drew away and walked off, leaving me to stew in the confusion of mixed messages and hopeless desire. I was excited that she wanted to go on the date with me, but if this minor exchange told me anything, it was that this was my last chance to fix everything that was broken between us.

twelve

. . .

"WHEN WAS the last time you bought her anything?" Kim asked as we stood in one of Mari's favorite stores, Tiffany & Co. I needed a girl's perspective for today's gift trip, even though my sister was not someone I would call a girly girl. I'm pretty sure she had nothing girly since high school. She did wear a vegan leather jacket, but that doesn't fall under the girly category.

I scanned through all the silver jewelry, trying to figure out what Mari already owned from this place. "Aside from food, not since her last birthday."

"Yep, you are well overdue."

We studied all the aisles, holding stunning pieces of jewelry for something worthy enough to give as a gift. Gift giving had to be the hardest thing. No one was easy to shop for, except Chris or Logan. Just give them each a burrito from Moe's and they were good. They never expected much. Mari was impossible. Get the wrong thing, I was in the doghouse. Get the right thing, I would round second base in no time.

"Doesn't she like butterflies?" Kim asked.

"Dragonflies," I corrected.

Pointing downward into one of the glass cases, she looked at me with a smirk. "There, bada-bing, bada-boom."

Sitting on a fancy white pillow laid a small silver dragonfly necklace, all sparkly and shiny enough to make me squint. Its wings were lined with little white jewels, probably diamonds or whatever gemstones. I am not a geologist. The price bolstered that it was probably something a girl would swoon over, and I didn't remember seeing Mari with a necklace like this, so the chances of her having it were slim. Unless my powers of observation worked for shit.

"Awesome." I scooped it up.

"You really want to spend that much money on it?" Kim asked, eyeing the price tag.

"Why not? She's my girlfriend."

"Yeah, but… I don't know. I don't see the purpose of gifts like this."

"That's because you're not normal."

She gave me a stare, squinting her eyes at me. "Just buy the damn thing and let's get out of here."

I flagged one saleswoman over to me, who smiled and wrapped up the necklace. Blasting out the cash, I handed it to her to complete the purchase. I took it, grinned, said thanks, and followed Kim out the door into the well lit jungle we call the Broadway Mall.

"Happy?" she asked. "Can we go home now?"

"You're driving, so it's your call."

We walked by a few strings of shops, mostly brand stores I never cared to learn or wanted to. We stepped onto the moving stairs to descend to the first floor. A few food kiosks selling sweets and health food shakes waited patiently at the bottom, sitting outside a few more stores with people coming and going. The large fountain wasn't too far from here, just a quick right turn and there it was, spouting out six small shoots of water surrounding two much taller ones. I never understood the purpose of fountains in a mall, I guess it was an 80s thing.

As we stepped off the escalator, Kim sharply turned left, looking down the west side strip of stores. "Wait for me by the fountain, I have to do something first."

"Why am I barred from coming with you?"

"Because it's none of your business, that's why," she said bluntly, taking off. "Just wait for me, I'll be back in two minutes."

"Fine," I huffed.

She swung around the escalator. "I'll text you! Don't wander too far."

Rolling my eyes, I blew air from my cheeks, making my way toward the fountain. I could get something from Annie's. They had good cinnamon pretzels. I hadn't had one of those in forever, with a kiwi-apple slush…

"Fancy seeing you here."

I turned around and there was Ashley, circling around me with her hands behind her back, leaning in like a tigress, jacket tied around her waist and a Joy Division t-shirt on. If I ever found out she actually listened to Joy Division, I would seriously need to rethink my position on her. I already was at this point.

I grinned. "You're popping up a lot lately."

"I've always been around." She stopped in front of me. "You just never noticed me before."

Looking down at the bag in my hand, her eyebrow raised. "Is that for your girl or for that other one I saw you with just now?"

"Uh, that's my sister." I chuckled uncomfortably. "So yeah, it's for Mari. I'm taking her out Friday night."

"Well, I wish you luck."

"Yeah, right."

"I mean it," she recanted. "If she makes you happy."

The invisible lines crease across my forehead. There was no sign of snakiness or intent to sabotage. She seemed genuine, but why? Why were these conversations so awkward for me, and why the fuck did she care?

My eyes glanced at the pulsar logo running across her black shirt. "So, Joy Division, huh?"

"Hell yeah," she practically shouted, her hazel eyes lighting up like a full moon. "I love those British fuckers."

"You know what happened to Curtis, right?"

"Yeah, 23 years and he wanted to end it all. Kinda, sad but," she shrugged, "his choice, right?"

"They're one of my favorite bands." I raised my chin. "What's your favorite song by them?"

"I'd be lying if I said I didn't love Love Will Tear Us Apart." She squinted in thought. "But I've always been a sucker for Dead Souls." With a sudden smirk, she tilted her head. "You quizzing me or something?"

"Well yeah, got to make sure you're not a poser."

"I guess I have to be extra cautious around you then, huh?" She popped out her hip, tossing her hair to the right. "Same question."

"Fair enough." I sighed. "I guess it would be Atmosphere for me. It just kind of…"

"Takes you away?"

Shifting my gaze awkwardly, I raised my eyebrow. "Uh, yeah. Exactly."

My stomach felt all fluttery inside, like I was afraid of doing something wrong. If we are getting technical, I was doing something wrong, talking to Ashley Carter when I was explicitly threatened not to. This should have set off all the warning bells in my head, but it wasn't. I didn't care about any of that right now. I didn't know anyone who liked Joy Division other than Logan. It was exciting to know we had that in common.

"Now that I've passed the test," she tugged playfully on my sleeve. "Can I show you something?"

"Hm," I looked around, "should I steer on the side of caution here?"

"No, you asshole!" She grabbed my arm. "Come on."

"I didn't say yes." I said, as she dragged me onward through the mall.

"You don't have a choice." she turned to face me with big, puppy dog eyes. "Please?"

"All right," I said. "Since you said please."

We walked toward one of the mall exits, tucked down those little one way strips. Pushing through the doors, we came along the sidewalk across from one of the parking garages. I followed her off the curb as we walked along the building around to the left. She didn't let go of my shirt for even a moment.

"Where are we going?" My curiosity was swimming with endless and dangerous possibilities. Where did a girl like Ashley Carter like to go?

"It's a secret." She looked back at me. "No one else knows about it, so you better not run your mouth."

"Not even Wes?"

"Especially him."

Ducking between one of the large bushes, she turned down an alley where a line of stores shared a shipping zone. There were dark green and black dumpsters against the walls and a tall standing garage door where trucks would back up and drop off shipment. A few grey doors lined the walls that lead to some stores in the mall, or at a least that was what I assumed.

Ashley let go of my arm in front of one dumpster. Kneeling down between two green ones, she nudged in closer. I looked down to see what the hell she was doing. There were a ton of boxes smashed up toward the far back against the wall.

"You got gremlins in there or something?"

"Gremlins?" She pressed her lips together and blew air through her teeth, making an almost shushing sound. After a few moments, I could hear cute tiny meows echoing from the depths of the boxes. A few kittens came stumbling toward her, crawling all over her lap.

There were four of them, all big-headed and unable to keep their balance for very long. A small gray cat came out after them, her yellow eyes looking at Ashley for some affection as she brushed against her hand to get a scratch behind her ears.

"Hey, mama," she said as the cat purred like a motorboat.

I don't think I could hide my surprise. This was the last thing I would expect a girl like Ashley to be doing on her downtime. Visiting stray alley cats behind a mall? That just didn't fit her character description, unless it was just a work. Her entire demeanor, her reputation, the rumors and the assumptions, everything. The more I spent time with her, the less I believed any of it.

One kitten scrambled over to greet me, falling on his side. I scooped him up and looked at his marble eyes, pointed whiskers and big Batman ears. He bared his little fangs at me before breaking into an uncontrollable purr. "They live back here?"

"Yeah," she said. "I know someone who works in a store that leads back here. She found them and wanted to get rid of them but I told her I'd take care of them, if she kept her mouth shut." Ashley pulled out a can of cat food from her black and white bag and peeled it open. The grey cat hunkered down to feast as Ashley placed it in front of her.

"Why don't you take them to a shelter?"

"Fuck no! She'll sit in a cage while her babies get adopted out and she rots in there her entire life! These little guys are free, they should stay that way."

"All right, take them home then."

"Yeah right." She scoffed. "My mom finds a family of cats living with us after working for three days straight. She'd flip her shit! Plus," she added, "Wes stays over sometimes and he's allergic to cats."

"Shit, he is? I should keep one on me at all times then." I put the kitten back on the ground. Her talking about Westley flashed some of the most recent memories back into my current thought patterns. "Why are you still with that douche bag?"

"Same reason you're going on a date with what's her face."

"That's totally different. She's not an asshole."

"She isn't? She's pushy as fuck."

The need to defend Mari's position flared up like I was building up a sweat. Mari was a lot of things, but she wasn't a hot-headed asshole like Wes. She rarely yelled, never physically attacked me unless I asked her to, and didn't have a mouth filled with dirt. But the more I thought about it, the more I was noticing how Ashley may have that impression. Mari had a way of making me feel small, like my opinions didn't matter. My indecisive nature seemed to irritate her to no end, and she had a way of making me do things, even after I'd written them off. But she was nowhere near Wes' level of assholery. That was where Ashley had it all wrong.

"Listen," Ashley breathed. "If you have something to say, say it to my face, all right?"

"I have nothing to say to you."

Observing me, her eyes narrowed a bit at my comment. "You got Breakfast Club Syndrome, don't you? With me."

"I got what?"

"Breakfast Club Syndrome. You can't let anyone know we're talking or your world comes crashing down."

"What about you?" I asked. "Are you telling people… well, I guess you are."

"What people?" she went back to scratching mama cat behind the ears. "Amber is my only real friend. The rest are just white noise. They wish they knew me like she did… or like you."

Like me? I didn't have time to wrap my head around that one, not without complicated psychology textbooks for me to reference. She focused her full attention back to the cats, letting them tumble and purr between her fingers and on her lap. "These guys keep me grounded. I hope they make it."

"You're doing okay by them and they look happy. You're like Catwoman only, less psychotic. They'll be fine."

Her eyes scrunched into her cheeks. Clearly not understanding anything I just said, but it was only for a split second. "You don't really think I'm what people say I am, do you?"

Waiting for a moment, the uneasiness in my stomach took a sharp turn as I tried to think of something to say. "Why do you care what I think?"

"I don't know," she mumbled, with hesitation in her voice. "I just do. It bothers me if you'd think that… I mean, we're kind of friends, right?"

A nervous chuckle escaped me. "So, we're friends now?"

She pushed me. "Shut up, you fucker!"

The force only threw me off a little. Recovering my balance, I attended to one kitten in a friendly game of chewing off my finger. "I don't think anyone who takes care of dumpster cats in the back alley of a mall could be a psycho bitch without a heart."

"Damn," her head snapped back in a sudden burst of laughter. "Is that what people are saying about me? I thought it'd be much worse."

"I can think of something worse."

She pushed me again, but playfully. "That's probably the nicest thing you have ever said to me."

"You're welcome."

We just hung out with the cats in silence, distracting ourselves with their innocent cuteness. Really, I was trying to distract myself from what I was doing… what was I doing? I was kind of flirting here, now, and almost every time I saw her. It was subtle and could be rationalized as annoying or just a way to get her off my back, but it wasn't. It was playful, and I did it entirely without trying, like I was acting on instinct. Did I like her? I guess I sort of did. I mean, she wasn't how I thought she was. Despite the frenzy of Poison Ivy thorns attacking my insides, I wanted to know more about her.

"It's nice… hanging out with you."

Ashley looked at me with a smirk. "Aww, are you getting all mushy with me?"

"No, I'm just saying," I glanced her way, "you're different, more than I expected you to be."

"Oh yeah? How so?"

"Well, for starters, you are a legit Joy Division fan. One of the greatest post-punk bands of all time."

"Hell yeah."

"And," I added, "you like the Breakfast Club."

"No shit! My dad educated me on all the classics." She shouted, "Anyone who doesn't like that movie is a fuckin' idiot!"

"Smart guy, raising you right."

"Yeah, he was pretty awesome…"

Her chin sunk toward her chest, as if there was something she had said that she never wanted to speak of again. Her fingers found that knitted bracelet around her wrist, running over the tightly wound strings of the pattern.

Was awesome… that would imply he was gone, erased from her life. Despite a desire to dig deeper into the person who was Ashley Carter, I wouldn't press it. Clearly, this was a side she rarely let anyone see. Maybe even her mentioning him was validation enough that she thought whatever this was between us, some fractured mishmash of a relationship. It was worth divulging secrets to. I got the impression she told me more than she even told herself, and I would not be an asshole to her for it.

As her eyes slowly came back to me, that spark of sadness was vacant from her. "You're totally a Brian, but an Andrew too."

"I am a brain and, technically, a jock." I nodded, "Something I feel strange agreeing with."

"Why is that strange?"

"Most brains aren't jocks, or at least, they don't want to admit it."

"Well, you aren't most guys, are you?"

I tried to hold back an automatic grin, but couldn't bring myself to press the pause button on my facial muscles. Ashley came up on her knees to face me, her hands settling in her lap as she shook the few freely falling kinks of hair from her face. "Who do you think I'm most like?"

Her posture was in full alert mode, like a meerkat looking across the African plains. It was adorable, so much so, I didn't think I could even stop myself from smiling even if I tried. It was tough to pinpoint her personality into a single Breakfast Club member. She had the Bender attitude, the awkward innocence of Ally, and the stuck up presence of Claire. That she felt she had to live up to how people saw her made her more like Andrew and Brian, both unable to think for themselves and just doing what people expected them to do. Wow, I really was like Andrew and Brian.

I saw mostly Ally in her, a manipulator, but also just someone who wanted anyone who would take a chance to look, to see who she really was. "If I say Claire, are you going to hit me?"

And she did, without wasting a second. Her hand came straight across my shoulder, hard but with no real ill intent. I raised my arm to defend myself, snickering quietly to myself from her reaction. "Fuck Claire, that self-entitled bitch."

Recovering from her attack, I lowered my arm once the onslaught ceased to threaten me. "She's the smartest one. Not book smart, but she knows the truth of it all."

Nodding, Ashley carelessly grinned. "Yeah, you're right. High school bullshit, she has it all figured out."

Placing the kitten that was scampering on my lap back down with their mother, I stood from the ground. The little critters scurried around her, pawing at her stomach for a good ol' mouthful of milk. I wiped some of the loose rock and other unknown littering of the alley from my jeans as Ashley stood and retreated from them, as well. I could tell she didn't want to.

"So," I said, "when are we coming back to check on these little gremlins?"

Her head shot around, staring at me with a clear, unexpected expression. "You want to come back?"

"Yeah, why not?"

"Yeah, sure." Her face brightened with surprised relief, like I would suddenly tell her to fuck herself and just leave. "I thought you'd think this was stupid or something."

"Not at all. It's your secret, right? It'll be our unspoken thing."

Did I really just call it that? An unspoken thing was Quill and Gamora, which could only mean one thing. Was it that? It was something. Something enjoyable and perhaps even desirable. It was like I was playing Duck Hunt and couldn't keep my Blaster steady when I was around her, shooting blankly into the sky while she laughed with every shot missed, but always willing to give me another chance.

"Unspoken only by you." She grabbed my hand and pulled out a Sharpie from her back pocket. "I'll keep you posted."

She scribbled something on my arm. "Here's my number. Shoot me a text so I have yours."

"I hope that's washable."

"Hm," she grinned, "you'll find out, eventually."

I looked at my arm, seeing the digits staring back at me. This should have felt wrong. A girl that I kind of liked was giving me her number. Me. A guy with a girlfriend who I was desperate to keep. It shouldn't be a big deal. She said we were friends, and I agreed with her. We were... friends, or at least, calling it that. I didn't know what it was, honestly. But it was innocent, right? Innocent and unspoken, which sounded so wrong on so many levels. I shouldn't be making excuses. I would tell Mari, I had to. Just maybe after our date. I didn't want this to screw that up, too.

Plugging her number into my phone, I texted her, hearing her phone bing with a message of her very own. She pulled out her newspaper covered cell and looked at the screen, grinning to herself. "Hello to you too. I'll let you know when I plan on swinging by again."

"I'm honored to be a secret keeper of kittens."

She smirked innocently. "God, you're such a nerd."

"You like that I'm a nerd."

That grin never left her face as she moved past me, grabbing on to my sleeve again. "Come on, your sister's probably wondering where you got whisked off to."

thirteen

. . .

WE WALKED BACK into the mall, toward the spot where I was supposed to meet Kim. I was kind of hoping she wouldn't be there, but to my not surprised self, there she was arms folded, sitting on an outcrop of brick by the fancy fountain. She pushed herself up and walked toward us, shifting her gaze from me to Ashley. "I was afraid you got kidnapped, and I can see I was right."

Ashley smiled momentarily at that, looking at me. I raised my hand to Kim. "Ashley, this is my sister Kimberly and vice versa."

"Wow, you sure know how to introduce someone, don't you?" Politely extending her hand, Kim smiled. "Nice to meet you, Ashley, who I have heard nothing about."

"Likewise." Ashley shook her hand. "Although I think you went to school with my brother."

"What's your last name?"

"Carter. But his last name is Smithson. Two different dads. "

"Oh yeah! Dimitri? He's in California on a scholarship for football, right?"

Ashley nodded, taking a casual step back. "That would be the one."

"God, yeah, he was funny." Kim shrugged with a momentary grin.

"Always cracking jokes in Spanish class, mostly in terrible Spanish. You'd think I'd remember he had a little sister."

"Well, we don't entirely look alike. I got 2."

"Older?"

"Yeah, Ty is the oldest. He lives in the city working for some acting company. Slacking off as my mom likes to say."

Looking at Ashley, I adjusted my glasses. "I didn't know you had brothers."

"Well, you never asked, so why would I tell you?" Ashley looked back to Kim. "You never told me you had a sister. I had to find out for myself, seeing you walking with some girl in the mall. I thought you were a player."

"Ha!" Kim practically fell backward. "Pete can't handle more than one thing at a time, let alone another girl."

"He does always try to make excuses for himself, doesn't he?"

"That's an understatement."

Raising my shoulders, I sneered, "I'm standing right here…"

"This is something you need to hear for your own good." Ashley teased. "Just another minor part of our unspoken thing, right?"

She waited for me to say something as her hazel-green eyes watched me expectantly. I could do nothing but match her smile, feeling my cheeks rise as it slowly spread across my face. For a second, I forgot Kim was even there. Shifting her balance, Ashley's head bounced from one shoulder to the other, still waiting for something to fall out of my mouth.

"I should get out of here," she finally said, smiling politely. "It was nice to meet you Kim."

"You as well," Kim replied. "I hope you'll be kidnapping Pete more often."

"An open invitation, I'll take it." Turning back to me, Ashley reached out and pinched my arm. "See you around, Andrew."

"I'm Andrew now?"

"Totally pulling an Andrew." she backed away, slowly releasing my arm from between her fingers. "Catch ya later."

"See ya."

She turned around, slowly being swallowed up by the foot traffic the mall endured day after day. The farther she got, the faster my anxiety came flooding back. College applications, baseball, my relationship with Mari barely hanging by a thread. It smeared my vision, something Ashley clearly had the ability to wipe away. I never realized how weightless I was around her, like she was more than enough to think about when we were together. The only thing I could think about...

When she was completely out of sight, I turned back to Kim, who had this incredibly conniving grin on her face.

"What?" I asked.

"What? What, you say?" She grabbed my arm. "To the car, short stack, and I'll tell you what."

The car ride home was a little awkward. Kim could not stop smiling and it was creeping me out. What really sank in was that Kim had met Ashley. I guess the fact that I was spending time with the one person who was shaking up my life, especially with Mari, was a little messed up.

"So," she glanced over at me from behind the wheel, "Ashley seems pretty cool."

"She's nice, I guess."

"Nice? Is that what you call it?"

"Well, what would you call it?" Curiosity had gotten the better of me. Kim could call me out on so much shit, it was impossible for her not to speak her mind. Even with Mari, she always told me how she saw it, and sometimes I have to admit that she called it straight despite my utter lack of acceptance. I could tell that Ashley had left some sort of impression on her during the five full minutes they had spoken.

"It doesn't matter what I call it," she answered, lurching the car forward, "but I can tell that you're trying to feed me some bullshit with that 'she's nice' response."

"I'm not feeding you anything."

"Buttshit, bullshit, bullshit!"

We lazily rolled through a stop sign before she floored it across the intersection. Classic Kim. She always had a heavy foot.

"Are you trying to get us killed?"

"Oh, stop trying to change the subject," she blurted. "I've seen Ashley before on campus. She's dating that asshole Westley, right?"

Shit, I forgot Wes went to the same school as Kim. He was a year or two younger than her, but it didn't even occur to me she might have occasionally seen Ashley there. The thought of Wes and Ashley raised my pulse a bit. He was a no-good-son-of-a-bitch, but she held on to him. For what? Yeah, he liked to ride fast and had that whole bad boy thing going, but come on. I know she had a mouth with a comeback for anyone who tried to throw something at her, but he put his hands on her, maliciously. That was not cool.

Maybe it had to do with her dad. I wasn't sure what happened, but he wasn't in her life anymore. Daddy issues can cause a total mess of unnecessary complications. At least that was what Arrested Development wanted us to believe. It was hard to know how to react to family drama, as mine was so cookie cutter. I doubt my parents even knew how to curse. Makes me wonder how they ended up with kids like us.

"Wes treats her like shit, he's such a douche bag."

"Oh?" There was a slight inflection in her voice. "And you know this how?"

Kim glanced my way a few times while trying to keep the car on the road. I saw what she was trying to do. I paid attention when I had to, which was less often than I wanted it to be. All right, it was really my fault; I didn't have to step in between a rock and a hard place. Stupidly, I did, and now, I couldn't avoid it even if I tried. Not that it was entirely unpleasant, and the rock wasn't so hard and impenetrable as she first appeared to be.

"I just know."

"You seem to know a lot about her, and yet you never brought her up before."

"What, you need to know everything that goes on in my life?"

Taking a deep breath, I tried to settle my defensive rage. Why was I getting so angry with her? Kim knew how to pull stuff out of me, and it had been bothering me more so than usual. I hadn't told her anything about Ashley, and that was probably why. I just needed one person to be in the dark so I could pretend like I had some make believe control over it.

"She's just a friend."

"Who are you trying to convince here, Pete?"

Holding onto the bag with Mari's necklace, I stared down at the grey box that encapsulated it. I did like Ashley. She was different, but that didn't change how I felt about Mari. I loved Mari.... or maybe love wasn't the right word. I wasn't sure what it was right now, but I knew I wasn't ready to let her go. That had to mean something, right? That had to say something about how I felt about her.

"Mari is important to me."

"Did I say she wasn't?"

The muscles in my neck tense. "Stop trying to bounce this around, like Pong or some shit. I don't need this right now. Especially from you!"

She shook her head, releasing a breathless smile. "You are the king at avoiding the obvious, Pete."

Her eyes focused on me as the red shine of the traffic light reflected off the windshield. "When are you going to wake up?"

fourteen

. . .

KIM LEANT me her car for my date with Mari. Yeah, I could drive, I just didn't have a car. My parents didn't buy Kim a car like most other parents do, but then again, she never asked for one. Through work and not spending her money, she bought herself a used one, but it was hers. Even if I wanted a car, I would never ask for one because my parents would shake their heads at me and say, "If your sister can work hard and buy her own car, so can you."

I was almost at Mari's house and already my palms were sweating all over the wheel. This was my last chance. I didn't want to say I was desperate, but fuck it, I was. The thought of losing Mari was like losing a part of my identity. Maybe it was because we'd been together for the last two years, or maybe it was that I really loved her or maybe I was completely insane and just had a hard time letting go of things, even when it felt like my arm was going to fall off if I didn't.

Too much was changing too fast. With high school coming to a close, I wasn't as excited to leave as she was. The thought of going to college scared the shit out of me. I was smart and got good grades, but did I really want to resign myself to one thing for the rest of my life? Work toward something that I might not even end up doing?

My dad never went to college, and he regretted it. My mom went for teaching but had not once worked as a teacher. Kim was a workaholic and college was a fucking mountain to conquer, so where did that leave me? Just standing on the edge of one of the biggest, most expensive decisions that most kids my age had to fall into or never have a chance to. Was I selfish if I didn't or stupid if I did? I had no clue.

So here I was, trying to hold on to the only thing I thought I had all figured out, my relationship with the first girl I had ever really cared about. Cared, why am I using the past tense for that? I care about her; I... love her... whatever that was supposed to mean for a high school senior who couldn't decide for himself.

As the wheels conked and creaked inside my head, I couldn't help but think about sitting in that alley at the mall, letting those cute little kittens meow and use my legs as a jungle gym. Ashley was in her element, watching those balls of fur play and fall all over each other. It was good to have that time to not worry about how my life would turn out. She had given that to me unknowingly.

What if Kim was right about how I felt about her? Nobody could know the answer to that but me, and holy shit, I didn't know who the hell I was half the time. Great start to a life with no direction.

Driving up to Mari's abode, I saw she was already waiting for me. Her hair was up in a ponytail, which she rarely ever did. She fixed the ends of her dark plaid purple dress as it fluttered against her leggings. I smiled as she opened the door, settling into the seat with a groan.

"My dad is in rare form tonight. I figured it was safer if I just waited for you outside."

"Well, thanks for that." I smiled as she closed the door.

She looked good without being too dressy. That was something I really liked about Mari. She was a girl, acted like a girl mostly, but never flaunted all that superficial shit that most girls did. She never wore a ton of makeup, never overdressed or took four hours to get ready. Aside from the assortment of colored nail polishes she owned and alternated on a weekly basis, she was far from high maintenance.

"We ready to roll or what?" she asked.

"All right. Let's drive." I pulled away from the curb and set off down the road of blinding obnoxious street lights toward our destination.

"So what's on the agenda?" she asked.

"I was going to take us to the Hitchcock double feature, but… I think we should just gun it to 88 and see where the future takes us."

"That sounds enticing."

"Which one? Hitchcock or the future?"

She grinned. "Don't we need a Dolorian to go back to the future, though?"

"There are no rules when it comes to breaking the space-time continuum."

"Oh, I doubt that very much."

Glancing at her, she held a permanent smile on her face that I hadn't seen in months. We were playing around again, something we did so much in our early days together, but rarely did now. It was fun and relieving, if I am being completely honest. It was right for me not to give up, because this seemed right. I wanted to ride on this high for as long as humanly possible. I just hoped Mari did, too.

"Well, just so we don't screw things up too bad, let's just stick with Hitchcock." She said, reaching for my hand between the seats.

"Safe but still enjoyable." I grasped the top of her hand, reaching my fingers to the inside of her palm. Her skin was so soft and I could tell she used that lavender lotion she liked so much.

This was going to be good for us. I could feel it.

The parking lot wasn't jam packed, but I still had to park toward the back. Roosevelt Field was a vastly larger mall than Broadway was. Sitting on one of the busiest roads on the island, it was practically the size of three football fields with restaurants, a movie theater, and probably over 400 stores.

My phone buzzed in my pocket as I stepped out of the car. I looked at the screen and saw a few texts, all from Ashley. Not bothering to read them, I stuffed my phone back into my pocket as Mari came around the car. "Let's go in before it gets colder."

She hooked her arm through mine as we made our way to the theater. My phone buzzed again, but I ignored it. I would have to shut that off the next chance I got. Nothing could distract me from Mari, not even Ashley. Too much was at stake here. It was going well so far, no matter how much of that was purely an illusion I made up in my head. It was now or never. I had to make this work, and I *would* make it work.

There was more of a line than I thought there would be to get in. These classic movie nights were a once a month gig at this place. I guess Hitchcock was a pretty popular name, even now. Luckily for me, I bought tickets early. Walking up to the counter, the guy manning the station in his Regency Theater polo shirt looked as thrilled to be there as it was to watch paint dry.

"Line ends that way," he yawned rather lazily, cradling his head in his hand while pointing down the standing patrons waiting to get in.

"I ordered tickets already." I pulled out my phone and popped open the APR code for the tickets, flashing my screen for him to see.

"So did all these people waiting." He looked out at the line again. "You still have to wait until they're done cleaning for the showing."

"How much longer will that be?" I stared at him while I stuffed my phone back in my pocket.

"I don't know, but not too much longer, I would think."

"You work here, don't you?" Mari butted in, folding her arms across her chest. "Can't you ask someone?"

"We'll wait." I looked at Mari. "It's no big deal."

Widening her eyes, she looked like she wanted to argue, but didn't press it. "Fine."

We reached the end and began our vigil with the other moviegoers. Mari shifted back and forth where she stood. Clearly, the chill of the evening air was getting to her. I took off my hoodie and draped it over her shoulders. She slipped her arms into it, smiling at me. "Thanks."

"No problem." I dove my hands in my pockets and held the small velvet pouch with her gift, sitting snugly in the corner. Fishing it out, I figured now was as good a time as any to give it to her.

"I got you something," I said as I held out the small gray bag containing her necklace. "Happy early birthday."

She gingerly took it from my hand. "You didn't have to get me anything."

"I know, but I wanted to."

She poured the contents of the bag into her palm. The little dragonfly landed perfectly on top of the nestle of silver chain, glinting in the humming theatre lights, standing out amazingly against her tan skin.

"Oh, Pete, it's so pretty!"

She took it, wrapping it behind her neck, clasping it securely before letting the little dragonfly fall against the décolletage. Rubbing the pendant between her fingers, she admired it for a few moments before looking up at me. "You really didn't have to."

"I guess that means you like it?"

"You know I like it."

"Then it was worth it." I smiled, admiring it against her skin. "It looks good on you."

"You're so sweet."

Standing on her tiptoes, she brought her lips up to mine and kissed me with silent appreciation. She stayed there, leaning her head and body against me as we stood in the evening air. I wrapped my arms around her, rubbing my hands up and down her back to stimulate some warmth between us.

"This was a good idea," she whispered.

"Why, because you got a necklace out of it?"

"No, you jerk." She gave me a little headbutt.

I squeezed her tighter to me. "You're right. It was a good idea."

The line moved inch by inch toward the entrance. We followed it together, me not letting go of her as she stayed leaning against me. The buzz of my phone went off a few more times before we reached the door.

God dammit, I have to turn that off.

Mari didn't seem phased by it. I hoped she didn't notice. As we walked inside, she pulled out of my arms as we made our way toward the concession stand.

"Your phone was buzzing like crazy," she mentioned. "I'd check it if I were you."

I shook my head. "It's nothing important."

"It might be your parents or Kim. You better check."

We got to the counter to order and Mari looked up at the menu. "A medium popcorn and a red slush please."

Fishing in my pockets, I pulled out my phone and looked at the screen. All from Ashley. Without even bothering to look at the messages, I held down the power button on the side, waiting for it to turn off.

Mari glanced at me. "Anything wrong?"

"No," I shoved it back in my pocket, "just guy stuff."

She shook her head, already forgetting about it. "Did you want anything?"

"You ordered for me already, didn't you?"

"No way, that slush is all mine!"

"All right, all right." I smiled. "Just get me another slush, blue though. I can't stand the red ones."

"Which is the reason I got it." She flagged the counter girl over again and asked for another, but the far superior flavor. "You can share my popcorn."

I grabbed my wallet to lay some money on the counter, but Mari pushed my hand away. "You drove and got the tickets. I'll get this, okay?"

"I won't argue with that."

We grabbed our food and made our way into the theatre. Some cheesy slides of random movie trivia flashed across the screen as we scouted for seats. I never enjoyed sitting close to the screen, so we always sat in the back. Most of the seats there were unoccupied. We shuffled our way through the folded chairs before sitting down in the middle of a row. Mari hung up my jacket behind the chair and got comfy.

I put my slush in the cup holder next to my seat. "I'm going to run to the bathroom before this gets started."

"Well, don't take too long."

"I wouldn't dream of it."

She smiled at me as I exited the aisle and made my way to the bathroom. I didn't want to waste too much time. The movie was starting in fifteen minutes, but that was fifteen minutes of time with Mari that I didn't want to waste. Rushing into the bathroom, I emptied my tank at one of the wall lined urinals, washed my hands and slammed the back of my hand against the power button of the wind tunnel hand blower thing.

Taking a quick peak in the mirror, I tossed a few loose strands of dirty blonde hair back against my head. The raised eyebrow of a white image of Hitchcock himself stared up at me from my black T-shirt. When I was about to watch the genius at work, I had to represent. I didn't look half bad, not that I did anything special from my usual routine, aside from getting rid of any premature stubble from my face. I was all for facial hair, but I was not ready to embrace it.

Anyway, I pushed my body against the door, swinging it open. I never enjoyed touching the handles of a public bathroom after I washed my hands. The dirtiest place in a public bathroom was the door handle, not the floor or the toilet seat, as most people were led to believe.

Stepping out into the lobby, I pulled out my phone, wondering if I should turn it on and see what Ashley was so frantic about. No, she had to wait. The last thing I wanted was to read something and spend the entire movie thinking about responding to her. It was better if I didn't know what she wanted and just deal with it later. This was Mari's time, not hers.

I wiped the remaining dampness from my hands onto my jeans and headed toward theatre three.

"Peter."

My head jerked to the left at the sound of my name. Amber was standing there with her arms folded and her body tense. She was wearing dark skin-tight jeans and an almost copper colored jacket, her dark hair resting against her shoulder.

A shallow pit formed in my stomach as I gulped down some stale air. "Amber, what are you doing here?"

She walked up to me. "Ashley needs to talk to you."

"Ashley's here?"

"She's been calling and texting you, but you haven't answered."

"Because I'm kind of busy right now."

"Look, she won't tell me what's up, so will you just come and talk to her for, like, two minutes? Please."

Her eyes darted around my face as if this was a last resort for her. I didn't really know Amber too well, but I knew she wouldn't have come in here for Ashley just because. For a second, I kind of felt bad for her. Ashley obviously knew what I was doing, and she found an excuse to make Amber feel guilty enough to come find me. I should have just walked away, but damn me and my inability to leave well enough alone.

With a sigh, I nodded. "Two minutes, that's it."

"Thank God." She grabbed my arm and pulled me down toward the double doors of the lobby.

Ashley was there, pacing, with her dark hoodie and hair bouncing at her shoulders. The moment she saw me, her mouth drew into a scowl and she walked over with such determination, I thought she was going to slap me.

"Why won't you answer your phone? I've been texting and calling you for an hour!"

"Well, hello to you too." I sighed, already regretting coming out here.

"Ash, what the hell is going on?" Amber was more determined to get this over with than I was. Looking at the door, I wanted to get back in there as quickly as possible. If Mari caught me out here with these two, she'd flip out. I probably should have just told Amber to fuck off, but goddammit…

"Wes saw us Pete," Ashley blurted out, drawing my attention like shit did to a fly.

"Where?" I asked.

"At the mall the other day."

With a huff, I looked around the parking lot, thinking he was going to pop out of nowhere and knock me out. "What, is he stalking you now?"

"What were you doing together at the mall?" Amber asked.

"We didn't go there together," Ashley confessed, "I just ran into him."

"Did he follow us?"

"No, he saw us with your sister." Ashley hesitated for a minute. "I knew he would be there."

Pressing my palms into my temples, I ran my fingers through my hair and turned away. She knew he would be there, what the fuck was she doing? Why would she talk to me if she knew Wes was trying to find an excuse to beat the shit out of me?

"Ash, Wes is getting out of control." Amber said, "You need to tell someone."

Ashley ignored Amber's warning. "Pete, I'm sorry, okay? I got the feeling he was going to do something. I just don't know when or where, so I had to warn you before he turned up, especially here with your girl."

"What the hell were you thinking? You knew, *you knew* he was meeting you there!"

"I told him your sister recognized me from campus. He doesn't know we did anything."

"*Did anything*?" Amber's eyebrows raised. "What exactly did you do?"

"Nothing," I harshly interjected. "We did nothing!"

The dark starless sky reflected in my glasses as I stared up at it, being the only thing I could do to keep myself from strangling her right there on the sidewalk. This wasn't a game. Why was she playing with fire, or better yet, why was I letting her?

"Look," I brought my head back down, forcing myself to look at her, "Unless you do something about Wes, I can't talk to you anymore, Ashley."

Rolling her head back, Ashley chuckled a little to herself. "Come on, Pete–"

"No, you don't get how fucking serious this is, do you? I don't know what imaginary world you're living in but, no. I can't anymore. I'm sorry."

"Pete's right, Ash," Amber added. "You need to go to the police."

"No! I am not doing that!"

"Tell your Mom then!"

Shrugging, Ashley's gaze dropped to her feet. "She doesn't even know I'm still seeing him."

Amber took a few steps back, her eyes widening. "You didn't tell me that, Ash. She doesn't even know he stays over at your house when she's not home?"

"Fuck no," Ashley shook her head. "She'd flip out."

"Ash, I can't believe you right now." Amber turned and walked away a little, leaving me and Ashley standing there.

"He was pretty pissed. I just wanted to tell you. You know he knows where you work, so don't close if you can avoid it. And don't walk home alone, okay?"

Shaking my head, I closed my eyes at the vastness of this ever mounting situation. "Should I get on the list for Witness Protection? Geez, Ashley." I backed away from her. "I'm going back to enjoy the last date I'll ever have before Wes beats the ever living shit out of me."

Turning back toward the door, I was ready to get the away from her. Mari would probably be wondering where I was by now. I reached for the door handle, but Ashley grabbed my arm and pulled me back around. "You're just leaving?"

"Fuck off, Ashley!" I pulled my arm away from her. "You came here, knowing why I was here in the first place, to tell me this now? You couldn't wait, you just had to crash my date with Mari."

"This has nothing to do with that."

"Are you fucking kidding me? *Of course it does!*"

She took a step back, Amber rejoining the fray of my onslaught.

"Obviously Wes is way more fucking important to you than anyone else, so until you get that shit under control, I am done with this! Don't come near me, don't text me or call me. I am done!"

"That's not fair, Pete."

"Neither are you dragging him into all this!" Amber added.

"I didn't drag him into anything. He dragged himself in."

Throwing my hands up in disbelief, the pulse in my head beat against the arms of my glasses.

"So all of this is my fault, then? What a fucking surprise. Maybe I shouldn't have done it. Screw me for trying to do the right thing then. Maybe I should have just walked away. Let him beat you fucking senseless, so at least then, he'd be arrested, and you'd finally wake up to the shit storm you've created for yourself and everyone around you. God, how selfish are you?"

Ashley's eyes glazed over, her face still. I must have struck a chord. About fucking time. I hope she felt bad because she should. It was clear she was using me after all, for whatever sick pleasure she got from making Wes go insane with jealousy and seeing my life in danger. Fuck her.

"Pete…"

That voice just sent an arrow through my chest. I turned toward the door, seeing Mari standing there. Her mouth hung open and her eyes squinting in disbelief. "What are you doing?"

"Nothing." Amber grabbed Ashley by the arm. "We were just leaving."

"You're a piece of shit, Pete!" Ashley shouted as Amber dragged her away unwillingly.

"Don't bother me again!" I pushed out as they left.

"Fuck you!" That was the last thing I heard as they disappeared down the sidewalk toward one of the many mall entrances.

Standing just outside the door, I could feel Mari's stare drilling multiple holes into my body. I took a deep breath, shutting the anger up to let the uneasiness climb aboard this shit show of a night. I looked at her, waiting for what would come next. She tapped her purple nails against the glass door, waiting expectantly. "So that's your guy stuff, then?"

I sighed. "Look, that was about Wes."

"I don't care what it was!" she snapped.

"It's done now, okay? I told her to leave me alone. For real this time."

"So, she wasn't leaving you alone before?"

"No, not exactly…"

We just stood there, staring at each other. I was a complete asshole, not just for completely ruining my date with Mari, but for yelling at Ashley the way I had. There was no way I could apologize to either of them. I was a shitty, lying boyfriend and a lousy, selfish friend. Nothing was more true to me now than that.

"I know I screwed things up, so if you want me to take you home, I will."

Mari gritted her teeth before relaxing her jaw. "I came here to see a movie and I'm going to see a movie. With or without you." Holding open the door, she waited for me to say or do something. "So what are you going to do?"

If she was staying, I had to stay, no matter how awkward it was going to be. Who knew, maybe I could salvage this, but judging from the death stare expression on her face, I was her ride home and that was the only reason she was allowing me to even entertain the idea of staying. So, why waste probably the last time we'd spend any sort of time together that would remotely resemble a date?

"For what it's worth, I'm sorry."

"We'll talk about it after. Or never," she said, waiting for me to move. "Are you coming or not?"

fifteen

. . .

EVEN WITH HITCHCOCK TO distract us with angry birds, it was hard to ignore the tension that was lingering between us. I made no attempts to breach the chasm. There were a few smiles brought on by visual distractions. As soon as she realized who she was next to, it would just erase. Remembering the reality of it was worse than seeing a school teacher getting her eyes gouged out by birds, apparently.

The car ride home was quiet. I asked her if she wanted to talk about it and she just gave me that stone cold look. You know, that murder hawk stare that just screams open your mouth and you'll die? Yeah, that sort of look. So I kept my mouth shut and my mind focused on if she would ever talk to me again after tonight. When I got to her house, I pulled up next to the curb. She opened the door before the car even stopped.

"We'll talk tomorrow." She said, shutting the door, leaving me in silence as I watched her walk up to the house.

If she meant that, I couldn't tell. Driving home, I felt like a zombie. Walking into my house and going upstairs to my room was all a blur. As I jumped onto my bed, lying down to stare at my ceiling fan spinning around and around, I waited for the night to be over. Closing my eyes, I could not get the image of Ashley's face out of my head. She was selfish... but so was I. A selfish, lying asshole.

Taking out my phone, I pushed it on to the onslaught of half a million texts and missed call notifications. Scrolling through the typed words Ashley had sent sunk me deeper into a hole of misery.

> I know you're with your girl, but I have to tell you something.

> Earth to Pete!

> Seriously, it's important. Call me back!

> I'm sorry I'm botherin u. Please stop ignoring me.

> It's about Wes, CALL ME!

> Pete, where r u?

> I'm comin to find you before Wes does.

> I don't want to get u in trouble with Mari.
> Please come out for just a second. PLEASE!!

Dropping the phone to my chest, I released the longest, most hopeless breath toward the ceiling. Now I had definitive proof of how much of a jerk I was.

Monday after school was another blur. Standing on the burnt orange dirt between second and third base, I barely heard the bat explode the ball straight toward me until someone shouted, recognizing that I was somewhere else.

Red spinning lines came at me faster than I could move to catch it. The ball hit the tip of my black tarnished glove before it settled into my palm. Squeezing it, I drew my arm back and sent it to Tom, who was standing on the pitcher's mound. He caught it, raising his shoulders at me as if to say, "What is up with you?"

I didn't talk up a storm about our date, so both Chris and Logan got the idea that things did not go well. Mari told Rina about Ashley's and Amber's star appearance as the official date crashers of the night. Rina asked me about it on the way to chemistry class, and I kind of told her the gist of it. I wanted to forget it even happened.

"So, are you still together?" Logan asked me at lunch.

"I don't know… I mean, we didn't say we weren't."

"Then you are. It ain't over till someone says it's over."

He might have been right, but it didn't feel like it was. Mari barely even attempted to talk to me the entire day, despite seeing her a handful of times in passing or in the lunchroom. And Ashley, she was nowhere, not even with Amber.

"Pete!"

Another shout propelled me out of the storm I had been feeding in my mind since last Friday. This time, I was far less ready. The ball came skipping at me from the ground, passing right under my legs. I launched myself backwards to catch it, but only fell flat on my face in the dirt.

Smooth Pete. Real smooth.

Luckily for us, this was only practice and not an actual game.

Dante ran off third to come over to me. "Dude. you okay?"

I rolled over, wiping the specks of orange and red from my glasses with my dirt streaked uniform. "Yeah, I'll live."

He patted me on the shoulder as I stood and practice resumed with my head more in the game. Another hour of position drills and batting, and the team called it a day. I grabbed the bat bag and slung it over my shoulder as we headed down the field toward the locker rooms. Chris was talking to a few guys, so I was glad to not involve myself in any riveting conversations if I could avoid them. Once we were almost at the locker room door, he turned and lifted his head toward me.

"You'll come too, right, Pete?"

"Where?" I asked.

"I'm having a party after the game on Saturday." Tom adjusted his cap on his shaved head.

"Eh, I don't know."

"Oh, come on, you need to take your mind off things, especially after what happened," Chris encouraged me.

"What happened?" It completely intrigued Tom.

I shook my head. "Oh you know, screwing things up, the normal shit I do daily."

"With Mari in particular," Chris added.

"Ouch," Dante chimed in.

"You have to come," Tom pleaded. "The more people Rina knows that are there, the better chance she will too."

"Dude, why don't you just ask her out already?" Dante asked. "We're graduating soon and who knows what A-list school she'll be whisked away to."

"He's right." Chris snapped his fingers before meagerly punching Tom in the arm.

Tom had a crush on Rina since junior year, even though they barely spoke. The problem was he was so incredibly shy around girls, it far surpassed normal. I wasn't sure if Rina liked him, too. It was hard to read her sometimes because she was comfortable around me and our core group of friends. But when any outsiders tried to weed their way in, she was a mouse hiding behind Mari or one of us. Tom was a decent enough guy and I would back him up, but how do you get two shy people to talk to each other?

Believe me, we tried, and it failed again and again.

"What if Mari goes too? She'll go if you go, right?" Tom asked.

"I don't know if she even wants to know I exist right now."

"Wow, that bad, huh?" Marcus's eyebrow raised.

"Look, I'll ask Mari," Chris patted me on the back. "If she goes, Rina is sure to go too. She follows her everywhere."

Sucking down my disappointment, I gripped the strap of the bat bag in my fist. "I'll ask Mari, okay?"

Chris looked at me. "You sure, man?"

No, I wasn't sure, but I couldn't walk around like an ostrich with my head up my ass for the rest of the week. If I didn't talk to Mari now, I would never talk to her again. This would be a good icebreaker.

I hated leaving things just floating in the air, all quiet and lacking stability and direction, like a seed that tickled your nose and caused you to sneeze. It was there, soundless and light enough to not exist, but the second it made contact, it screwed your entire world up. It was time to swallow the hard medicine and deal with the problem that I willingly created.

"I'll go talk to her. I should."

Blowing air out of his mouth like a whistle, Tom held up his fist to celebrate this minor victory. "Pete, I love you, man."

"Don't get ahead of yourself here."

"Yeah, Pete might ultimately fail, and then you'll have to ask Rina yourself." Dante chuckled, his eyes squinting from his uncontrollable grin.

Tom shook his head, rolling his eyes. "That would be terrible."

"For you or for her?" Marcus added.

We reached the doors of the locker room and piled inside. I put the bat bag in the supply closet and looked at the clock. It was a little past five PM, Mari would just be getting out of band practice. If I hurried, I could catch her on the way to the bus. Not even bothering to take off my practice gear, I grabbed my bag and headed out of the gym toward the side of the school where the late buses lined up for their nightly pick ups.

The buses wouldn't leave for another 45 minutes, but Mari never waited till the last second to board. She was a full-time work on the bus kind of girl. Super fan of confined spaces, so the bus was an ideal place for her to be comfortable and productive.

I got to her bus and peeked inside. It was empty aside from the bus driver, who was busy with his headphones on and his nose in a book. I didn't see any sign of her until her voice hooked me like a baited fish. "Pete." Mari was standing on the sidewalk with her hair down, backpack and sax case in her hand. "What are you doing here?"

For a second, my throat dried up. I was kind of hoping I wouldn't find her, so I wouldn't have to do this. She acknowledged me at least, but her presence sent my heart working overtime with the amount of nerves my body was producing. I wanted to reach for my water bottle on the side of my bag but thought that would be a desperate move, so I swallowed uncomfortably and mustered up my reasonings.

"Tom is having a party on Friday night. He wanted to invite you and Rina."

"If he wanted to invite me, why didn't he just ask me himself?"

"Because I said I'd ask you… because I wanted to talk to you."

She swallowed hard, adjusting her hold on her sax case. "About the other night?"

"Yeah, and I don't know. Just to see how you were."

Her face relaxed, dropping her guard a bit. "Yeah, I'm doing okay. How are you doing?"

I shrugged. "Pretty shitty, but that's my fault."

She breathed a heavy sigh, looking away. "Yeah, it is."

Chewing on my bottom lip, I tensed my entire body before breathing out the words.

"I am sorry, for lying to you again."

We waited there, letting other school goers walk past us, talking and laughing, or complaining about all the things teenagers in high school thought mattered in their lives. No one appreciated silence anymore. Something always had to be playing in the background 24/7. It took a lot of self-awareness to take stock of everything that was happening around you, to pay attention and not keep yourself distracted. I was so distracted lately, so fucking distracted by everything.

I was not ready to give Mari up, but I got the sense she was ready to give up on me. Why couldn't I just let her go?

"Are you going to go too?" she finally asked, breaking the silence of my insolent thoughts.

"I might, I don't know yet."

"Well, I'll go if you do. And Rina will go if I go."

An uncontrollable smile sprang across my face. I tried to expel it as fast as I could without giving away my sudden excitement. "Yeah? You'll come?"

"If you want me to, yeah."

"Yeah, I want you to. I wouldn't go if you're not."

"And Tom wants me to go because of Rina, right?" Her head tilted to one side, reminding me of Ashley a little.

"Well yeah, I mean he'd invite us anyway, but being friends with Rina is an added incentive."

"Why doesn't he just ask her out already?"

"I don't know if he ever will."

Mari shook her head and smiled. "Oh god. The things we do for people."

The rock that had weighed me down since our disaster date chipped away, just enough to realize that Mari didn't entirely hate me.

"So, Ashley…" she said. "She's your friend now?"

I wasn't sure how to respond, except with the truth. "Yeah, we were sort of, but I told her we can't anymore. You know, with Wes breathing down my neck. She's a little delusional about the whole thing."

"That makes sense. Probably smarter that way, you know?"

"Yeah, but she's… she's not as terrible as people say she is. Not really."

Nodding, Mari pressed her lips together. "She could use a friend like you then."

Her words surprised me. I wasn't sure what she meant by that. Was she trying to tell me something or just sarcastically poking fun at me?

"I have to go," she breathed, "but I'll see you tomorrow."

Mari walked past me, stopping just before the curb and the open bus door. "Tell Tom he's got nothing to worry about, okay?"

"Sure, he'll be relieved."

"Text me later?"

I leaned against the bus just outside the door. "Yeah, sure."

She stepped onto the bus and made her way down the aisle. I wasn't expecting a goodbye kiss; she talked to me at the very least. She seemed okay. Maybe we were okay. As I walked back down the sidewalk, I couldn't help but feel disappointed. She seemed to forgive me. I didn't deserve it, and that comment about Ashley needing someone like me. What did that mean?

The thought of Ashley brought Wes back to my mind. I didn't think he was ballsy enough to come after me on school grounds, so I would take the bus home, just to be safe. Reaching into my pocket, I remembered I was still wearing my baseball uniform. I wanted to text Ashley, tell her I was sorry for being so shitty to her. I'd talk myself out of it once I got back to the locker room. Maybe it was better to wait until I saw her again. She should know I was sorry, even if she wanted nothing to do with me ever again.

sixteen

. . .

I MET up at Logan's house before heading to the party. Hopping on our skateboards, we cruised our way down the street, weaving in and out of parked cars, only stopping to cross any semi-busy streets. Tom lived on the other side of town, closer to Chris and Mari. We could have drove, but it was a pleasant night and skateboarding was our preferred mode of travel. My new board was breaking in nicely, smoothly transitioning to my weight without it seeming sticky or stiff.

"This is going to be interesting." Logan nodded as we waited for our chance to cross one of the major roads.

"I seriously think Tom is throwing this party just to make an excuse to talk to Rina."

"Well, it sure isn't for the game you lost today." Logan grinned. "I heard his dad got some promotion or deal or something."

"They throw parties for every pointless thing imaginable."

"They're kids living in adult bodies. What can you do?"

The walk sign flashed us across and we hopped on our boards to cruise along the white grid lines. We had a few more blocks to go before hitting our destination.

"So," Logan glanced, "Rogue or Shadow Kat?"

Jumping off the curb, I let out a sigh as my board landed on the street. "In what context is this X-Men related question?"

"In whose pants you'd want to get into."

"Of course." The streetlights reflected off my glasses as we pushed forward. "Well, I think the risk would be far less with Shadow Kat. Rogue could wear gloves, but there's always a chance something would screw up and then I'd be a vegetable."

Logan got a chuckle from that one. "Catatonic dude, completely catatonic."

"Who'd you go with?"

Kicking off the sidewalk, Logan joined me in the street. "Rogue's way sexier than Shadow Kat."

"Shadow Kat could levitate. Air sex is not possible with Rogue."

"No leverage, man. Air sex sounds like a chore."

I turned to him, eyes squinting in amusement. "How much have you thought about this?"

"Enough to know I wouldn't have a chance in hell with Rogue. Kitty seems way easier. She'd be all over me, no problem. Just have to put on the charm."

"That's not charm, dude…"

We rode up to Tom's house. All the lights were on and there were cars cramming the driveway and the curb out front. Tom's house was pretty big, not as big as Mari's, but bigger than mine. I wasn't sure what his parents did for a living, but they had money, clearly. The front of the house was sandstone, two floors growing up into a brown roof.

They had a garage that could probably fit two SUVs, but it housed the family motorboat in the off season. Strings of lights ran from the back of the house to the fence. A grill and a smoker adorned the large wooden deck that lead out from the living room.

Grabbing up my board, I threw it into my backpack as we approached the door.

"Do we just walk in?"

"Probably."

Before we knocked, Tom opened the door with an enormous smile on his face. "The last of the crew to arrive."

"We took the long way."

There were a ton of people, not enough to fill the entire house, but a decent amount. All the team was present, and some of Tom's younger brother's friends.

Tom motioned in bland disgust at the glass sliding door leading to the yard. "The adults are in the backyard, so try to stay inside. I don't want any of those drunks walking in here being all shit-faced."

"Sounds like YouTube material to me," Logan suggested with a smirk.

"Are Rina and Mari here yet?" I asked.

"Yeah, Chris is here too. They all came together a half hour ago. They're around here somewhere. Enjoy guys." Tom went back to socializing like any decent host.

"I need to take a leak." Logan shifted forward as we integrated ourselves.

"Have fun. I'm going to find Mari."

"Good luck, man." He side-stepped around toward the bathroom as I walked into the dining room hallway. There were a few people hanging around, talking and drinking out of those famous red cups. Passing them carefully, I followed it around toward the back of the house, still not seeing her silky black hair and coke bottle shape anywhere. As I turned the corner, Rina almost collided with me.

"Pete!"

She looked frantic. Her eyes were pretty wide from either crashing into me or the fact that it was me.

"What's the rush," I asked. "Are you okay?"

"No, I mean... yes..."

She looked around, a sinking feeling crept into my stomach once her eyes found me again. "Listen, Pete..."

A sudden motion behind her caught my attention, forcing me to look up, so I did. What I saw froze time for a few painful seconds.

Chris and Mari were there, lip locked at the end of the hall, his hands wrapped around her waist and hers pulling at the back of his neck to keep him there. I swore my heart stopped and hit the floor, trying to halt this memory from forming in my head.

"Pete..." I heard Rina's voice faintly beneath the ringing in my ears.

Mari's eyes opened from the sudden passion they shared, seeing me standing there caught in the crosshairs of betrayal. I turned tail and beat it down the hall. Everything was blurry, people's faces, the floor, my hands reaching for the door to get the fuck out of there. My pulse was moving so fast, I could hear it both in my chest and against my skull at the same time. I was seething, not at them, but at myself. I knew this was coming, not Chris sucking face with Mari, but the end of what we had. Holding onto hope that it wouldn't be was stupid, immature beyond my own fathomable belief.

"Pete, wait!" Chris' voice hit me like a punch to the stomach.

I tried to cross the lawn, but his hand reached for my shoulder to stop me. Looking back, I stared at him with vicious intent. "Don't! Just... don't."

"Pete!"

And there she was, the human embodiment of both my pain and my joy for the last two years. I couldn't bear to look at Mari, but I forced myself to. I deserved this punishment, and I would not hide from it.

Her lips trembled with the hurt threatening her eyes. "It wasn't–"

"Wasn't what?" I snapped, my arms pleading in front of me. "Wasn't meant to happen? Is that what you were going to say?"

"Pete, come on–" Chris added.

"You keep your fucking. Mouth. Shut!" I shouted, pointing an accusing finger at him.

He backed off, right into Tom, Marcus, and a few others. Rina stood close to them, holding her hands over her mouth.

Running her fingers through her hair, Mari let her pitiful tears fall. "I didn't want it to end like this."

"But you wanted it to end!" I ran my hands through my hair, threatening to pull it out of my scalp.

"Come on, don't give me that bullshit! We both were holding on to nothing! I know you tried. I tried... but we can't keep doing this anymore. I'm tired, Pete. I'm tired of trying to make this work when it's not! It hasn't... for a long time."

"And this is how you decide to tell me! I love you! Don't you understand that!"

Shaking her head, tears fell down her cheeks. "In your world maybe, but not in mine…"

I just stood there, slowly absorbing her words as I forced air into my frantically shrinking lungs. My eyes were on fire. I couldn't focus on anyone else but her, despite more people coming out to see what the hell was going on. Right in front of me, Mari didn't move or blink as her sadness continued to flow. I wanted to hug her and shake her at the same time. There was so much messing around in my head, I couldn't tell which way was up.

I noticed someone stepping beside me, but I didn't bother to see who it was.

"Hey," Logan breathed, "go for a walk, man. I'll come with you."

"No." I took a step back. "No, I'll go."

"Pete…" Mari's desperate whimper turned me back to her.

Shaking my head, I continued my backward escape. "It's no sweat. I'll go. Have a great fucking night."

Turning on my heels, I stared down the empty street and left. How fast, I had no clue. I had to get out of there. I had to get away.

As I widened the gap between me and Tom's house, I kept my nose to the ground and my hands in my jacket pockets. I crossed one street after the next, only looking up to make sure no cars could crash into me, though I'd probably welcome it.

My pulse was still racing at 100 miles an hour, and I couldn't catch my breath fast enough. The anger rose and fell with sudden impulses to just curl into a ball and cry like a baby. I realized if I stopped walking, I would probably do just that, so I kept going.

Soon the rows of houses became strip malls and office buildings. The rushing sound of the train grew louder as I escaped into the busier part of town. Moving cars and the flashing of stoplights suffocated my ears and pulsed in my eyes. It only made me want to walk faster, like if I escaped any trace of society, it would be okay to just fall apart.

I crossed a street when I reached Main, not caring to look, but it was busy. How long I'd been walking, I had no clue. The scene of them replayed in my mind a thousand times, holding each other. Kissing each other. Nothing could snuff it out.

When I reached the other side, I passed a row of stores and restaurants. None of it looked familiar, but then again, I wasn't really looking. I was about to pass the last one when I heard someone calling my name.

"Pete. Hey, Pete!"

My feet stopped, almost like the voice forced them to. I turned myself around and peered up, seeing the stone shock on Ashley's face.

"Shit, are you okay?"

Shaking my head, I tried not to focus on her. "It's nothing. I…"

My face grew hot, like it was being forced into an oven. Pressing my hands against the sides of my head, I closed my eyes and turned away, keeping the emotional rise I had been holding at bay from revealing itself.

"Hey."

Her hands came down on my arms and tugged me around, forcing me to stare at her. She was searching all over my face.

"Ash!" I heard someone shout. Maybe it was Amber. I couldn't tell.

"I have to go."

"Seriously?"

Ashley glanced over her shoulder. "Yeah, seriously, okay?" She grabbed my arm tight and pulled me. "Come on."

"No," I shook my head, "you don't…"

"Come on!"

I had no will to stop her, so I let her drag me wherever it was she wanted to go. Stepping off the curb, we meandered into a parking lot and then to her car.

"Get in."

I did, crawling in like an injured animal. Shutting the door, Ashley walked to the other side and got into the driver's seat. My face fell against the cool glass of the window, staring at the blacktop as she pulled out of the parking spot and onto the road.

seventeen

. . .

THE NIGHT WAS FALLING, but no matter how dark it seemed to get, the light pollution that surrounded us never let anyone enjoy it. My numb hands rested in my pockets, not realizing I was digging my nails into my palms the entire car ride. Long Beach was about forty-five minutes away from Hicksville, and that was without traffic. I had no clue how long we were driving. We got to the party around eight o'clock and I left pretty quickly. So, it could have been pushing ten.

Closing my eyes, the instant replay of Mari and Chris pressed against the wall together was permanently cemented into the back of my eyelids. It was like a punch to the face, a swing that had been lingering over my head for months that had finally hit its target. Mari was right. We grew apart long ago, but she saw it and she did nothing. We both were hopelessly trying to keep our balance until one of us finally fell.

I didn't know if I was mad or sad or what; it was probably everything all at once. But Chris, fucking Chris… why? Why him? It could have been anyone else. He may have been caught up in the moment. I could see it on his face. Regret and utter distress. I'd forgive him. Fuck it, why should I? I should let him stew until he disintegrates into nothing.

"Hey, you in there?"

My head jolted to the right, Ashley standing there tilting her head to one side with the car door open. Her hood up over her head, hands in her front pockets. I didn't remember the car stopping or her getting out. I forgot I was with her for however long I was lost in my head. But now that reality collided with my memories, it sank everything, keeping my body tethered to the seat. There was nothing I could say. I just looked at her as she waited with calm patience.

Reaching down, she grabbed my sleeve. "Come on, grab your board and let's stay awhile."

Her fingers drew down my arm, pulling away from me as she made her way to the stairs of the boardwalk. I huffed hot air into the speckled lights, reaching back into the car to grab my skateboard. Dragging my feet, I looked down to make sure I was actually walking, like I had those ridiculously large cartoon barbells strapped to each of my ankles. Where were Popeye's spinach infused muscles when I needed them? Luckily, I didn't have to walk too far.

I could see Ashley had parked herself on the nearest bench overlooking the sand, leading toward the gently rolling ocean. People were still wandering along the coast. Some runners and dog walkers came into view, either across the wooden platform or on the beach. Ashley sat on the back of the bench, her feet swaying back and forth like she was listening to music in her head. I sat on the seat, leaning my board against the bench.

She nudged my shoulder as I sank back against its hard surface. "You want to talk about it?"

"Not particularly."

I stared up into the reddening sky, trying to make out the stars, other planets and civilizations where I would much rather be than here.

"Was she with someone else?"

Those words sunk my head down into my hands, pushing up my glasses so I could mash my palms into my eyes.

"That sucks, but it's not like you weren't expecting it."

I wanted to tell her to shut up, but I simply didn't care. She was right after all; I had seen it coming. She told me it would. Hanging her arms down over her knees, her eyes wandered to the ocean in front of us. The setting sun and the flickering lamp post light trickled through the springs of hair, escaping her hood, outlining her face and erasing any imperfections she might have been hiding. Guilt squeezed my stomach into a tight ball. The last time I saw her, I said some pretty shitty things.

"I'm sorry," I whispered loud enough for her to hear it.

She turned to me, almost bewildered, smiling awkwardly. "Why are you apologizing?"

"For yelling at you. For being a shitty friend."

With a shrug, she looked back out toward the sea. "You didn't mean it."

"Still, I shouldn't have… you were right about me, about everything."

"Breakfast Club syndrome." She spoke with a smile that I couldn't help but reciprocate. "You got a critical case of the stuck up Claires."

"That's the worst strain you can get."

"You should know."

Nodding, I laced my fingers together into a tight ball. "I should know or I should have known."

I looked down as I crossed my thumbs, one over the other. "I don't know why I was lying to myself. Fucking daydreaming."

"It happens to the best of us, don't beat yourself up about it." We sat quietly for a minute, just listening to the tide lapping against the damp coastline, waves gently rolling out to sea in the distance.

"I love coming here." She was calm, her voice relaxed as she stared out toward the horizon. "Here and the baseball field at school after dark. I can breathe a little better, think a little clearer even."

"Is that why you brought me here?"

She glanced at me, pulling a spring of hair from her face. "Just another secret to add to our unspoken thing."

I had to look away from her to conceal my uneasiness. This thing we had, it was an imperfect circle. I didn't want to understand it, but I wanted to at least get a better sense of what the hell it was about her that made me feel grounded. Even after being cast into the chaotic emotional storm that seeing your girlfriend kissing one of your best friends can create. "Hey, can I ask you something?" I kept my eyes on the ground.

"Go for it."

The innocence of her voice grabbed my attention, so I looked, even though she focused on the evening waves. "What's with you and Wes?"

She took a deep breath, letting go with a long drawn-out exhale. "It's complicated."

Glancing at my miserable self, her teeth rolled across her bottom lip before hiding them again. "He wasn't always an asshole. In high school, he was different. Then his mom left him with his drunk for a dad and... he got mean. Now he's just out of control. Doing shit for the wrong reasons. I guess... I thought I could save him."

My eyebrows raised. "You don't think that anymore?"

"Like I said, it's complicated."

We just stared at each other, waiting for something else to happen. I needed her to keep talking about it, for her to admit that she was just as afraid as I was to let go. Maybe I was tired of being alone in all this, like I was the only one struggling to accept how much life was about to change after high school. If just one person, one person, told me they felt the same... I wouldn't be so lost.

"So," she glanced down at her bracelet again with a relieving sigh. "What now?"

I didn't have the energy to push her on it anymore. She didn't have to tell me. Maybe I noticed it all along. That was why I felt like myself around her, but who knew? The state I was in didn't render clear scientific data about my teenage psyche.

"I don't know." I leaned farther back against the bench, throwing my head over the back. "I guess I should focus on college."

"Is that really what you want?"

She raised an eyebrow, looking impatiently at me like she appreciated how much I was trying to convince myself that the lies were true.

"It's what everyone else wants me to do."

"Fuck them. Who gives a shit what they want? What do you want?"

I shrugged. "I don't know. What kind of question is that, anyway? Does anyone really know what they want?"

"I do," she stretched her legs out in front of her. "As soon as I graduate, I am getting the fuck out of here."

My head popped up off the bench. That serious determination in her voice, she wasn't screwing around. She was going to leave and nothing was going to stop her. A small twinge of jealousy stuck in my throat, but only for an immature moment before I cleared it away. "Where are you going?"

"Anywhere. Everywhere. Any place but here."

I folded my arms across my chest. "And how do you plan on doing that?"

"My dad left me an inheritance. Technically, I could leave right now, but I promised my mom I would finish high school." She leaned forward, elbows on her knees, swinging her head toward the ground just enough for me to think she was remembering things she wished she could forget.

"So, he passed away, I take it?"

She didn't look up and hung in the aftermath of my words. "Yeah… when I was fourteen."

I folded my fingers together, looking down at my hands. "I'm sorry."

Before I got to know her, like really know her, I didn't think being vulnerable was part of her character. But here she was, clear as the night sky, capable of more human emotion than the average person. She wasn't even trying to hide how much mentioning her dad dropped her five hundred feet from the sky, unable to save herself from the misery it created. I hoped I would never have to see her look this sad ever again.

"He was such a cool person. Everybody loved him. Even my brothers. He was my hero. He used to say no one can tell you what to do but you. Sometimes I'm glad he's not around. Some daughter I turned out to be."

"Don't say that."

She glanced at me. "Why not? Because I'm such an amazing, upstanding person?"

"I didn't say you were upstanding." I averted my gaze for a second. "But you aren't a screw up."

"We're all screw ups, some of us are just better at hiding it."

I took a deep breath, breaking into a smile. "That's top notch Breakfast Club philosophy shit. Like when you grow up, your heart dies level excellence."

She grunted and leaned away. "Way to kill the moment, Pete."

"That's what I'm good at, apparently."

It was crazy how much the last rays of the sun remained trapped in her eyes. The buzzing lamplight coated her kinky curls and blended them into her face so naturally, she looked damn near breathtaking.

"It's not a bad thing, not now anyway." Adjusting herself where she sat, Ashley stared at me, her face lightening. "You should come with me."

"What?"

"When I finally get out of here."

I shook my head. "Are you asking me to or telling me?"

"Come on. What else do you have going on?"

I had to stop myself from blurting out an answer. At this moment, I would go anywhere with her. But I wasn't thinking clearly, not after what happened only an hour before. "Why would you want me to go with you?"

Her voice shrank a bit. "Do I really have to spell it out for you? You're kind of my hero."

"Bullshit."

"No bullshit!" She leaned back with her eyes squinting in offense. "You think anyone would have done what you did for me? You're fearless. You don't give a shit about the consequences if it means doing the right thing. You're like Batman, without the billion dollars and souped up shit. It makes you more real than anyone I've ever met."

Her words shocked me into another realm of awakening. No one has ever called me fearless before or said anything close to that scale regarding my character. Batman? Where did she pull that from? I mean, it was a hell of a compliment, and for a second, I didn't think she meant it. But her posture raised and her expression intensified.

There wasn't an ounce of uncertainty in her voice, not a single miscommunication in her words. She meant it…

"Batman, huh?"

Curling her lips, her head came to rest on her shoulder as she shrugged. "I may have stolen some of Wes's old comics. Unbeknownst to him." Her feet tapped on the seat's surface. "And I went back to your store, when you weren't working…"

"Holy shit."

"I didn't steal anything!" Her hands came down on her lap, voice raised and alert that her reputation might have led me to that conclusion.

"No, I didn't think that," I lowered my tone. "You don't owe me anything, you know that, right?"

"Stop being so fucking modest." She sat down on the bench next to me, closer than I would have expected her to. My skin prickled and popped like being caught in the freezing rain. I couldn't bring myself to look at her. I just stared at my hands plastered against my jeans as I rubbed the sweat from my palm.

"I'm flattered that you compared me to Batman."

"Well, it's about time someone did."

I leaned away from her to get a full view of her face. "Which one though?"

"There's more than one?" Her single eyebrow raised at her adorable ignorance to the world of comic book heroes.

I was sure my smile took up more than half my face. "We'll have to watch all the flicks one of these days. A Bat-a-thon."

"Yeah, I'd be down for that…. nerd."

She put her hand on my leg, barely touching my fingers. It wasn't in a flirtatious or get-in-your-pants kind of way, more in a comforting way. A reassuring sign that she wasn't going anywhere. If I was being perfectly honest with myself, I didn't want her to be away from me. Ever. My pulse picked up, keeping time on my neck. I wanted to hold her hand, but felt like it would be such a shit thing to do after everything that happened tonight, everything that was still happening. Even though I knew there was no me and Mari anymore, I was still bound to her somehow. I guess even now it still didn't feel over; I was still holding on.

"You're pretty fearless too," I said.

Ashley scoffed, rolling her eyes. "I'm not fearless. I don't give a shit, but that doesn't mean I'm not scared." I looked up at her, "I'm always scared."

A smile crawled into the corner of my mouth. "You keep surprising me."

"That's a good thing, right?" She raised that curious eyebrow again, which only drew out my smile more. She really was beautiful, way more than I've ever noticed before.

"I think so."

She held me there, locked inside her hazel eyes. For a second, I forgot why we were even here. The reason was becoming obsolete. I was grateful for it. If it didn't happen, I wouldn't be here, looking at her, talking to her, and enjoying her company.

She leaned her head on my shoulder. That spearmint scent hit me like I just skated into a brick wall. My mouth was so dry that no words would stick. What the hell was happening to me? I had just fought like a fucking lion to keep Mari because I loved her, and now it seemed like something big was about to happen. Something that was both so clear and so confusing.

Pinching my leg, Ashley shot to her feet and smirked. "All right, enough of this real life bullshit." She swept up my skateboard and stood in front of me. "Are you going to teach me how to skateboard or not?"

"You want to learn how to skateboard?" I smirked. "Are you sure about that?"

"Why do you think I brought you here? To watch the sunset? Fuck that!"

A light chuckle escaped my lips as I stood in front of her. "All right, but I won't go easy on you."

"Good." She smiled that brilliant smile as she handed me by board. "I wouldn't want you to, anyway."

eighteen

. . .

MONDAY. School. I wasn't nervous or eager to walk into the thick of whatever aftermath I was about to face. After that night, I didn't pick up my phone once. I must have had over thirty missed calls and unanswered text messages. I called out of work, which Dave thought was bizarre. Something was up, but it wasn't depression or anything like that. I was drowning in the night I had spent with Ashley. Nothing intimate happened… or maybe it did. A new intimate, something I never really had experienced before.

You think of intimacy and you think of anything physically pleasurable; touching, kissing, sex, and shit like that. Yeah, she had sat close to me, and I held her on the skateboard to keep her from falling. We ran into the icy waves before sitting together on the beach, wrapped in blankets she had stowed away in her car. And I held her hand as she traced along my fingers and up my arm. She had fallen asleep, and I carried her to the car, watching as the sun came up. When she woke up, we drove back with nothing to say or listen to except for the rush of the wind coming in from the windows.

She dropped me off, just smiling at me as I exited the car. I had closed the door with my skateboard in hand, waiting for her to pull away but not really wanting her to. It seemed like she was having a hard time leaving me, too. When she finally left, I watched until the car was out of sight. I stood there like I was dreaming, stuck between asleep and awake.

I had spent the rest of the weekend just sitting in my room, playing video games or catching up on homework. My parents questioned me when I didn't leave for work on Saturday, but I just told them I needed to use up my sick time or I would lose it before my next review, which wasn't entirely a lie. I never called out sick, so I could see the reason for their concern. I even looked over some of those college applications that were still on the dining room table. Even filled my name out on some of them, if for nothing else, to get my mom off my back.

I hadn't told Kim about what happened, though she sensed it. Aside from the many things that annoyed me about Kim, she was aware there was a time and place for everything. She had seen whose car I got out of and put two and two together. If she had asked, I'd tell her, but she didn't have to. Everything that happened, an entire book's worth of events, causes and resolutions, left the story of my night lasered in the reflection of my glasses.

Grabbing some books from my locker, I shoved them into my back-pack before sizing up my skateboard into my narrow coffin until it was time to leave. The halls were alive with the usual bustle, the last time to socialize before the bell roped them into another tireless seven hours of classes and school work.

"Pete!" I glanced around my locker door and saw Rina rushing over to me.

She was alone, the corners of her mouth pointed downward. I cracked a smile. "Hey."

She leaned against the neighboring lockers, shifting her stance nervously. "Where have you been? Everyone's been trying to call you all weekend."

"I've been… around."

"Logan said you didn't show up for work," she explained as I closed my locker. "You never call out. He was worried about you… we all were."

"I'm fine," I reassured. "Really."

"Really." Rina took a deep breath, letting her shoulders drop in a slump. "Are you sure you're okay?"

"Yeah, I'm good." My eyes strained down the hallway. "Is Chris around?"

"He's in homeroom last I saw him."

"Cool."

Slinging my backpack over my shoulder, I put a hand on Rina's arm. "Thanks for checking in. Don't worry about me though, okay?"

"Okay," she breathed, the unnatural wrinkles of worry cringing across her forehead. "I'll see you first period?"

"Yeah."

Before I could step away from my locker, she launched herself at me, squeezing me around my arms and chest. I didn't move, finding the support of her arms comforting. I wish I could have hugged her back, but she had me pinned against my body like Jean Grey at her worst. After a minute, she released me.

"You're one of my best friends, Pete. I'm always here for you."

"I know, Rina, and thanks. I guess I don't say that enough."

She smiled and made her way down the hall to homeroom. That reassuring gesture put me in a good place. I didn't think I took my friends for granted, but sometimes we all did. It was nice to remember who's on your side, and who's got your back, no matter what.

Making my way down the slowly depleting hall, I kept myself focused on the homeroom door. I didn't want to get distracted from what I was about to do next. Was I pissed the night I saw Mari and Chris making out at Tom's party? Heck fucking yes, I was. But after shutting myself off for a few days, my head wasn't so messed up. It would be wrong if I let Chris stew in the guilt any longer than he already had. A small part of me wanted him to suffer a little, but he tried to call and text me the most over the weekend, so it showed he was sorry. I wasn't one to let myself get carried away with punishment, of all things. Chris was my friend, and he had been for most of my life. I didn't want this to screw that up. It wasn't worth it.

I stepped into the classroom, looking down the lines of desks facing the chalkboard. Chris sat a row across from me and one chair shy. He was there, his head down, concentrating on whatever he was scribbling in his notebook. I walked past him, took a seat in my chair, and put my stuff down.

"Hey," I muttered.

I never saw anyone's head shoot up as fast as his. He dropped his pen with his eyes as wide as the Death Star. "Pete, shit... I..." He turned his body in his chair to face me. "I tried calling you."

"I know," I shifted in my chair, "I got your messages."

"Why didn't you call me back?"

"I didn't want to."

He nodded. "That's fair." Bouncing his sneakers on the dull carpeting, he looked just about ready to crack. He was always an anxious guy, so me ignoring him for this long was probably worse than Chinese water torture. He took a deep breath. "Look, I don't know what to say other than I'm sorry. She was so upset and I was just trying to be there for her and she just... I don't know what the hell happened."

"Do you like her?" It was a legit question. I mean, he liked her in the friend way, but was there more that I was too stupid to see? Wouldn't surprise me. He seemed confused and mildly offended by the question, shaking his head with his eyes squinted.

"No, no. I mean, she's my friend. I never thought of her like that before."

He held his breath, leaning in on his knees, which mildly controlled the shaking of his legs. Something about what he said annoyingly tapped at the back of my mind. He never thought of her like that before. I didn't believe it. This was supposed to be a forgiveness session, not pull more shit out of the closet. But he was still nervous, the relief from apologizing wasn't enough for him to get comfortable. Chris could never just hold on to something like that and not say anything, but he was with this.

With a deep huff, he rubbed his hands over his knees. "It was a one time thing. I would never fuck you like that, man. You know that."

Hesitating, I studied the tension he was trying to control in his eyes. "I don't know if I believe you."

He pressed his lips together as he came back up. "Look, Pete–"

"I don't feel like talking about this anymore." There was something on his mind, something that he was getting ready for, but my pulse picked up again and that feeling that I wasn't completely in control squeezed the air out of my lungs.

"All right." Chris sat back against his chair and I did the same, rearranging the papers on my desk. "Are you going to talk to her?"

I shrugged. "I have to. I can't just leave it where it is now."

"She was a wreck after you left. Rina had to take her home."

"Rina took her home, or did you?" I raised my brow in accusation.

"Hey, I was out of my mind after you left! I thought I was going to have a panic attack or some shit. I don't even know how I made it through the night."

The bell rang, pushing the teenagers into their seats and cueing the beginning of morning announcements. Less than three months before senior graduation, they added a new lunch special to the menu, and blah, blah, blah. My mind was elsewhere, now thinking about the impending conversation I would still need to have with Mari. I wasn't sure what I was going to say to her except how sorry I was for being such a shitty boyfriend. All the thinking dragged me through the mud of worry, but almost without willing it to be, it became the waves crashing on the sand. The boardwalk as night turned to day. The car ride home after something happened that never would have happened if all this didn't.

Another interruption, loud enough to push me out of my thoughts, moved everyone to their feet for the start of first period. I slung my backpack over my shoulder and headed for the door. Chris followed behind me, lugging his books in the crux of his arm.

As we stepped out into the hallway and turned left to head to history, I caught a glimpse of that kinky brown hair bobbing in the rush of traffic. The sight of her made me stop. Her arms wrapped around her books as she made her way down the hall. She noticed me in her stride, and as she passed, raised an eyebrow, smiling as brilliantly as she did when she left me in front of my house. We watched each other until she absorbed into the crowd. It was like she was moving in slow motion or something. She was different, or I was finally seeing her how I was meant to.

"Uh… Pete?" Chris' questionable tone barely took me out of the moment.

"Yeah?"

"You're grinning like the Joker over here. Without the murderous glint in your eye."

Turning to him, I squinted unexpectedly. "Really?"

"Yeah," he glanced down the hall where she had been swallowed up. "You okay?"

I wasn't okay, nor was I the same person who stepped outside of homeroom. I must have been crazy, crazy that it took me so long to realize what the hell was happening. Finally seeing through all the bullshit antics, the irrational enemies and flying fists. It was a total Scott Pilgrim moment. The signs were there. It just needed a second, so fast it was almost unnoticeable, to blow all that smoke away from my face and stop my eyes from burning.

It wasn't Ashley who was distracting me from Mari, but the other way around. I was missing what was right in front of me, daring myself to think it wasn't what it was. I didn't love Mari, or maybe I fell out of love with her and I was just telling myself I still was. If I was, it would feel like this strange sensation that I could jump off the highest building and still be okay. That no matter what the fuck I did to screw up my life, just being with her would fix everything… I had never felt that before. Not with Mari or anyone.

Just her.

"Yeah." I smiled. "Yeah, I think I'm okay."

nineteen

. . .

MARI WAS SITTING on the bleachers during gym class. She was alone, half paying attention and half not. She hadn't changed into the usual Hicksville Comets t-shirt and dark shorts, so she must have talked her way out of participating. I walked up to her, trying to hide my shivering nerves under my skin. She looked at me as I approached, her hair falling into her face as she swept it behind her ears. A faint smile rose and fell from her cheeks. She didn't seem happy or sad, just indifferent. There wasn't anything Mari couldn't handle, but I could tell from her inability to look me in the eye for over two seconds, that she was just as nervous as I was.

Sitting down next to her, I shook out my hands before leaning them against the metal bench. "Hey."

"Hi," she uttered.

I rolled my lips under my teeth, my leg shaking a little to give this unsettling pain inside my stomach some sort of outlet. I had to do this, but it scared me to have a civil conversation with her. It was easier when we just yelled and ignored each other. Why couldn't I just hate her like what couples do in the movies?

Because unlike what most teen dramas want you to believe, that's not actual life.

"I'm sorry," I said.

"Me too." She took my hand and looked down at our fingers. "I wasn't trying to hurt you."

"Do you like him?" It was a stupid question, even if she did. Who was I to stop her?

"Chris?" she asked. "Yeah, but not like that. We're friends."

Unlike Chris, her voice didn't skip a beat or carry any uncertainty. She was being truthful. "I don't know why I asked that."

"Don't worry about it, I'd ask the same thing if I was in your shoes."

We looked at each other, her brown eyes barely focusing on me. I wish I knew what she was thinking or what to even say to make her smile. Despite everything that had happened, I cared about her. I hated seeing her so conflicted and all because of me, because I couldn't let go.

I leaned forward, shoving my hand between my knees. "It scared me to let you go. I didn't want things to change."

"I know." She looked away into the field. "You've always hated change."

"But it's not the same anymore. I knew it and I still couldn't let go."

Shaking her head, she put her hand on my leg. "It's not all your fault, Pete. You tried, and I never told you not to. I don't know if I was just hoping it would get better or what, but... I should have just done this weeks ago." Her comforting hand slid down toward the metal blench. "I kept stringing you along and I'm sorry."

Before her fingers hit the bench, I wrapped them safely in my hand. "I ignored you. I was a fucking coward, and you were right. I saw it and I ignored it. You didn't have to tell me no." I held my breath for a second as she looked at me. "I am so sorry, Mari. For everything."

I could see a hint of sadness trying to escape from behind her eyes. "I'm sorry it turned out this way."

"It was unavoidable." I shrugged. "It just happened."

She smirked a little, breaking the tension knotting in my stomach. "You just had to throw in a quote from the Breakfast Club, huh?"

A breathless chuckle escaped my lips. I didn't realize I had done that. "There is never a wrong time for a BC quote."

She laughed along with me, returning the favor by squeezing my hand gently in reassurance. "Friends?"

"Always."

She leaned in and kissed my cheek, a long, drawn-out gasp ending this mass of nerves we both carried. Letting go of my hand, she stood up. "I have to get back to class. See you at lunch?"

"Yeah, sure."

Smiling one last time, she walked down the bleachers, leaving me there to sit and absorb everything that just happened. It was over now, officially. Mari and I were no longer a couple, after two long years of being one. As much as it had its moments, moments that made me want to hold on to her forever, the relief of finally letting her go made it a little easier to breathe.

I sat on the bleachers a little while longer. A few more people got up and made their way back to class, but this was my free period. There were still a lot of things speeding around in my mind, like Chris. He wasn't being honest with me, and that hurt almost as much as breaking up with Mari. I realized how weird it was going to be from here on out. If Chris did like Mari, like I think he did, how was I going to be around them?

The relief I felt from smoothing things out with Mari evaporated. This wasn't over, not by a long shot. Break-ups were a messy business, no matter how mutual they were. Mari was my first girlfriend, so this was all new to me and I wasn't looking forward to what the next few days would be like. But I had to deal with it.

After a few minutes of stewing in suffrage, I slid off the bench and made my way along the rows of shrubbery separating the parking lot from the field. Dragging my feet through the rocks of the walkway, I watched my sneakers take imaginative damage as I moved past the gate. A body turned the corner, almost colliding into me but stopping just before we made contact.

"Pete." Looking up, Ashley huffed loudly, placing her hand on her chest. "You scared the shit out of me."

I stepped back, realizing the frazzled look on her face. "Hey, you okay?"

"Yeah." She took another breath, but something was up. The usual smirk or eyebrow raise she always had for me didn't make it to the forefront. Her nerves kept her moving, whether it was her looking down at her purple Converse or rubbing her hands on her pre-ripped jeans.

There was a lot left unsaid, a lot of stuff that happened that neither of us could explain. I didn't expect the next time we talked one-on-one to be some magical Disney movie come to life, with birds and squirrels singing around us. Awkward was the wrong word to describe it though. It was almost like waiting for the inevitable.

"I uh… I really liked hanging out with you the other night." Geez, could I have sounded more idiotic? My uneasiness seemed to shake some weight off her shoulders as that smirk made an appearance.

"Liked?"

"What? You want me to break out a guitar and sing you a ballad?"

She chuckled, "I'd pay to see that."

"I'd probably pay too."

I joined her in her smile, feeling any tension ease up a bit as a cloud passed over the sun. With a sigh, Ashley looked at me, her lips pressing together before glancing down. "Look, we have to lie low for a while. Wes is..."

"Pissed?"

"That's an understatement." Ashley came back up to look me in the eye. "Just for a few days. You know? He doesn't know where I went and I don't need him to find out it was with you."

"Yeah, I know." I ran my hand through my hair, biting the inside of my cheek. "Was it worth it?" I'm not immune to insecurity, and I didn't want her to end up hurt because of me. That and I wanted to know if spending hours in Long Beach together was actually enjoyable.

Her hand rested on my arm. That half-cocked look sent my pulse racing, flooding my brain with more blood than it could handle.

"I think so. Just another addition to our little unspoken thing, right?"

I froze, unable to do anything but stare at her as she kept her hand on me. Ashley's eyes flashed expectantly, that eyebrow raising its arched head yet again before a half-hearted chuckle escaped her. "Come on, Pete. Lighten up."

Letting go, she backed away a step or two. I pulled at my shirt collar, like I was having a hard time breathing. "Sorry, it's been a weird day."

"I bet." Ashley tugged on my sleeve and we walked back toward school together. We stood uncomfortably close. Uncomfortable because I wanted so much to reach for her, but god, was I out of my mind to even think that. I had just officially ended things with Mari, and already trying to move on as fast as humanly possible. The second Ashley was not within a hundred feet of me, I'd be right back where I was before, stewing in uneasiness and lack of fathomable direction.

"I'm not cutting you off, Pete." Moving closer, she briefly leaned against me. "I'll be okay. Trust me, all right?"

I wanted to believe her, but I wanted to yell at her that nothing she had done before got Wes off her back, ever. She wasn't safe from him. As confident and capable as she was, I could tell she was talking this up more than normal. She was nervous, maybe even scared. Looking over her shoulder, waiting for a bomb to explode.

"I do trust you." my cheek twitched against the frame of my glasses. "It's him I don't trust." We got to one of the back doors of the school. Before she reached for the handle, I grabbed her by the wrist. She looked at me, her eyes squinting as her mouth dared to lash out, but refrained. "Promise me you'll call me or text or whatever. If I can't be seen with you, I want to at least be sure you're okay."

She nodded, "Yeah, sure." Her hand came on my own. "You worry too much, Pete."

"And you don't worry enough."

With a shrug, she leaned closer to me with a smile. "You like that about me though, don't you?"

My body shuddered as she drove me up a proverbial wall. "You drive me insane."

"Good to know." I dropped her hand as she grabbed the door handle, opening it while leaning once more in my immediate direction. "Text you later, Pete."

twenty

· · ·

IT WAS JAZZ NIGHT, and I sat on the front steps of the school with my buds draped around my neck, watching students, parents and the like shuffle up and down the steps into the building. In the two years I had been with Mari, I never missed a concert. It was her big night, but it tore me up deciding whether to go. We were technically still friends, but it didn't feel right. I was sure it was the combination of breaking up and this weird vibe that was coming off of Chris when he was around Mari. Plus, crushing hard on Ashley didn't help ease my anxiety.

Being slighted like that, as much as I wanted to just tie a rock around it and chuck it into a river to drown, wasn't easy. I couldn't just rip myself away from a relationship that I thought would last forever, even though that thought was incredibly naïve for a high schooler. And Chris, he looked at her differently. There was something there, something I never noticed before or was too stupid to. It made my stomach turn every time they were together, making it hard for me to be anywhere near them.

The lack of interaction with Ashley was eating away at me, too. I kept my word and forced myself not to be around her. We texted a few times, but she always gave me a one word response or nothing at all. I had to keep reminding myself that she'd talk to me when the ice age in hell finally thawed, but it was taking too long for my primitive teenage mind to bear. Rubbing my forehead, I leaned on my knees and looked up at the clouded sky.

"Hey," Chris' voice popped into my ear, "what's on your mind?" He sat next to me, his hands coming to rest against the stairs.

Raising an eyebrow, I glanced at him with a shrug. "Stuff."

"You coming in?"

"I don't know. It feels weird to sit there and not be with her."

"With Mari? Or… with Ashley?" The dark skin of his forehead raised as he waited for me to confirm his obvious suspicions.

I found it hard to breathe from the sudden onset of pain in my chest, hearing Ashley's name uttered by someone other than myself. I told no one about what happened at the beach that night. Any information kind of just leaked out in onlooker interpretations, mostly Mari. I guess I couldn't hide it forever; I was sure Chris was waiting for me to just forgive him already, so it heightened his powers of observation. Hiding any sort of emotion right now was impossible, even without speaking.

"Look man, I saw how you were looking at her after homeroom that day."

"Yeah." I sighed. "You caught that."

"You never told me what happened after you left the party. Did it involve her?"

Pressing my lips together, a tight ball rolled around in my chest every time I tried to breathe. I didn't want to say anything, not because I was embarrassed. Hell no. But it was no one's business but ours. Not breathing a word to anyone about it made it that much more sacred.

"All right, you don't have to tell me." Chris responded to my undeniable silence.

I shook my head, hanging my arms over my knees. "No, it's just… I don't know what it is yet, if it's even anything."

"But it is something to you." Chris looked at me more directly.

"Yeah, it's something."

"I remember when you first started crushing on Mari," Chris shook his head with a smirk, "you wouldn't shut up about her. But this time, with Ashley… it's different."

Fuck him and his ability to just pick up on the most random shit. I'd done it to Chris hundreds of times. It still never ceased to blow my juvenile mind. "Different isn't a big enough word."

Nodding his head, Chris patted me on the back. "I hope you figure it out. And when you do, you know I'm in your corner."

"Right, like you were with Mari…"

"Wha–come on, man."

A brash exhale shook out the obvious nerves riddled on his face. Chris rubbed the back of his neck, straightening his posture while meeting my unmoving stare.

"How long are you going to hold that over my head?" he asked.

"As long as it takes for you to tell me the truth."

More people were rushing toward the doors. It was almost time for the show.

"Seriously though," I whispered loud enough for Chris to hear, "if you like her, just tell me."

The words scraped the inside of my throat as they came out. Chris searched my face, eyes squinted in hesitation. The jealousy inside me bubbled up, but I held it down with the strength of a thousand suns. I had to shake this if I was ever going to feel comfortable around them, even if they never dated.

"I notice things too," I added.

With a nerve-rattling huff, Chris nodded slightly. "I guess I don't want things to change between us."

"They already have."

Chris sighed, looking me square in the eyes. "All right. Yeah. I like her. I have for a long time. But there was you and now," he brought his hands up as he crossed his feet in front of him, "she doesn't need that right now."

I had to bite my tongue. He liked her, even when we were together. Looking back, it was something I should have noticed. He always defended her, always had her best interests in mind with the problems we had. Being wrapped up in it all, my blinders were up on all sides. So many obvious things slipped past me, this being one of them.

Swallowing hard, I closed my eyes to suck down my immaturity, despite it leaving a foul taste in my mouth. I couldn't be pissed at him. How could I be bitter? If it would turn me into that kind of person, then no thank you. I wasn't good enough for Mari anyway, never was, according to her dad. Fuck me for feeling sorry for myself. I didn't deserve to.

"Thanks for being honest." I looked back out toward the parking lot.

"I wasn't trying to start anything. I didn't plan to do you like that. It just… happened."

"I get it. It's done. Just need to get over it and move on." I could feel him looking at me, not really sure how to respond. Did I have a right to feel betrayed? I fucking hope so. But I didn't have a right to tell him I would never have done that to him. If it was him instead of me, would I have been able to stop myself? I don't know.

"So, we cool?" Looking back at him, his eyes were wide in anticipation of my approval to resume our friendship. It would be different, but I was okay with that.

"Yeah, we're coo–"

Before I could finish my thought, Wes' dark booming sedan came rolling up to the front of the school, coming to a halt at the bottom of the stairs.

"Shit." I pulled my hands across my lap and got to my feet as Wes stepped out of the car.

He slicked his hair back. Baggy black jeans and a plain grey T-shirt formed the tight muscles of his arms. With his hands in his pockets, Wes stared me down as he approached.

Chris rose from the stairs, standing one step above me. "I got you."

Stopping on the platform below us, Wes scrunched his nose before leaning his head to spit on the stairs. "Where's Ashley?"

I shrugged. "I don't know."

"Don't give me that bullshit, you little punk." Wes climbed a few more steps to get in my face. "Where is Ashley?"

His smoker's breath fogged up my glasses. I may not have been shaking in my AirWalks, but my stomach was knotting up something terrible. Not because Wes was threatening to kill me, but because he was looking for Ashley, which meant she was in more trouble than I was.

Moving myself away from his hot breath, I drew my fingers into fists at my sides. "I told you. I don't know where she is."

"You better not be lying to me."

"Or what?" With his chin raised, Chris stepped down next to me. He was taller than Wes, and trying his best to appear threatening. "You'll kick my ass too?"

Wes drew his focus, a conniving smile painting across his smart-ass face. "You're lucky we're on school grounds. Otherwise, I'd drop you both right here." He shot back at me, his faded white teeth adding to his insanity. "You think you're tough shit, don't you?"

My blood was racing under my skin at lightning speed. "Why don't you just leave her alone."

Shaking his head, Wes leaned back as he pulled his hands out of his pockets. "What are you going to do about it, huh? You think I'll let you walk away again? You think the next time I see you, I won't knock you out?"

He got huge, pushing me back into Chris, who stood as immovable as a statue, keeping me from losing my balance. My eyes narrowed as Wes' smug face and menacing stare were all I could focus on. "Just go back to your drunk dad and deal with your own problems."

Shit. The practical me died a little inside as my threat widened Wes' dark eyes. Just the thought of him laying a hand on her turned me into someone I didn't recognize. Someone fearless. The person Ashley always saw in me.

"You're digging your own grave talking to me like that. Getting between me and her, and now, convincing her to stay clear of me? You think you can control her?"

"She's not mine to control. Or yours." I tried to sound as serious as possible, but it wasn't hard. The more I stared at his ugly mug, the more I wanted to punch him. He didn't scare me, not anymore.

The corners of his mouth curled up as he took a step back. "I'll find her. And then I'll find you." His finger came full force at my face. "You don't throw rocks at a man with a machine gun, punk."

With that, he backed down the stairs, not turning until he reached the bottom. I watched as he got back in his car, glaring at us before slamming the door and peeling from the curb.

"Damn, Pete. Who are you?" Chris asked, "It took everything in me not to break face with that douchebag."

I couldn't stop myself from breathing like an animal. My thoughts immediately went to my phone. Reaching frantically into my pockets, I pulled it out and turned the screen on. Scrolling through my contacts, I found Ashley's number and punched in a text.

Wes is looking for you. Where are you?

"Got any idea where she's at?"

I looked up at Chris, shaking my head. "No."

He glanced toward the door. "The concert has got to be starting up. You coming?"

I held my phone in my hand, waiting for it to breathe. It'd only been a minute and already I was panicking about why she wasn't responding.

"Look, come in with me. Maybe a minor distraction will jog your memory where she might be."

"Or I will just be freaking out the entire time–"

"Hey, man," he put his hand on my shoulder, "she'll text you back. If Wes had to come crawling to you to ask where she is, she's safe."

He was right, maybe. If nothing else, he was rational. I nodded; I had to at least try to keep myself calm. "Thanks for having my back there."

"Yeah, of course."

Grabbing my backpack, we headed up the stairs and through the doors into the main lobby. The auditorium was directly to our right. The doors were already closed and only a few stragglers still hovered on the outside. I could hear someone over the microphone.

I looked at my phone again as we approached the doors. Still no text from Ashley. My fingers danced across the screen again.

Please tell me you're safe.

As Chris swung the doors open, my eyes trailed away from my phone to center stage. The jazz band was filing one by one to their designated seats. The sounds of applause were steady as Mari passed the microphone, taking the second seat in the front. A tight ponytail swung across her back, wearing black dress pants and a white button-down shirt. She looked ready to kill it, holding her saxophone in her hand like a golden axe of fury.

Soon after she sat down, Marcus lumbered onto the stage, holding a large brass tuba across his body. I always forgot he was in jazz band. He was such a jock; it was hard to picture him doing anything else but football or baseball.

Baseball. The field.

My memory jogged back to the beach, sitting on the bench with Ashley as she stared out into the horizon.

"… the baseball field at school after everyone's gone. I can breathe a little better, think a little clearer even."

Nearly side swiping Chris, I busted the door open and crossed the lobby as fast as I could.

"Yo, Pete!" Chris shouted to me. "Where are you going?"

"I know where she is!" I raised my hand up, not bothering to glance back at him.

twenty-one

. . .

I WATCHED my feet leave the safety of the building as I stepped through the doors leading behind the school. It was a crisp early spring evening, and my sweat jacket was barely cutting it. They must have watered the field because everything was damp, leaving that thin layer of moisture still hanging on to the path. The baseball field was coming into view and, at a glance, I saw nothing but a line of parked cars pressed against the tall standing shrubbery separating the field from the parking lot.

Looking at my phone again, Ashley still had not texted me. If she wasn't here, I'd be screwed in finding her. Maybe she was at the beach or with Amber. God I hoped she was with Amber.

The team benches were coming into view. There was Ashley, sitting behind the fence to the right of home plate sucking on a vaporizer, puffing long plumes of smoke from her lips. She was wearing a black leather jacket and tight purple jeans with gray converse sneakers. Her hair was pulled back in a tight bun that sat on top of her head. I've never seen her with her hair back before. It made her face look so angular, her eyes standing out like searchlights. Red Beat headphones arched behind her head, breathing tunes into her ears that seemed to distract her from the world.

She was alone. Looking around, there was no sign of anyone else, which granted me a split second of relief. She didn't see me, her gaze fixed on the empty field in front of her. I watched her for a minute, trying to subdue an aching pinch in my chest that twisted so badly it wrung out my lungs. Fuck her for looking so beautiful and fuck me for ever forgetting that she was.

Approaching her slowly, I hooked my thumbs through the straps of my backpack. "Don't you know this is a smoke-free school zone?"

She jumped, wheeling around before taking an exasperating breath. "Shit, Pete…" She tucked her vaporizer in her jacket pocket, like she was afraid I'd see it. "What are you doing here?"

"I texted you."

Pulling off her headphones, Ashley grunted softly. "My phone is in my car."

"Wes was looking for you."

"And?" she barked. "Who cares?"

Squinting, I came up to the fence and sat on the edge of the bench. "What do you mean, who cares? He was ready to rip my head off, and yours too. I was trying to find you before he did."

She scoffed with a sudden grin. "Why do you care so much?"

Ouch. Every word that came out of her mouth was deflating my relief of finding her safe and out of harm's way. I went from wanting to wrap my arms around her to wanting to get the hell out of there.

"Sorry for worrying about you."

"You shouldn't." She finally looked at me, her eyebrow raised and head tilted to one side. I couldn't find the charm in it right now. She was jerking me around and being a full on bitch about it.

"Fine." I slid off the bench. "I'll get out of here then."

"No, no, you don't have to go." She sighed, dragging her head back to peer into the sky.

I stopped, looking down at my sneakers again as my tongue collided with my teeth. Forcing myself back on the bench, I kept my eyes to the ground, waiting for her to help me break my sudden desire to forget I ever cared.

"I've been avoiding him," she added. "If that means anything to you."

My next intake of air was a little easier to stomach after that. It meant something to me, but whether I wanted her to know that was a completely different matter. Thinking of that douche bag, I couldn't help but hear the snap of my skateboard breaking in half. She was avoiding him, sure, but she didn't say she left him.

"Is he coming with you after you graduate?" I asked, almost on impulse, finally plucking up the courage to look at her. "On your little trip."

"Fuck no." She leaned back as if trying to avoid me. "I wouldn't have asked you if he was."

"I don't know. Maybe you have some sick, twisted fantasy of watching him kick my ass or whatever."

"Stop being a dick, Pete."

"How is looking out for myself being a dick?" I asked, trying to bury my rage deep in the pit of my stomach. "Nevermind," I breathed, looking out into the field. "I'm sorry."

"Whatever."

"I don't want to fight with you."

"Then don't," she said with such disdain that I remembered who she was before I knew her. "You shouldn't even be hanging around me, anyway. If Wes catches you, you're in deep shit."

Leaning my hands on the bench, I turned to her critical stare. "Little late for that. Regardless, that hasn't stopped you before."

"Maybe it should have." She was trying to be tough, but she was moving from side to side and her eyes shifted away from me every second.

We sat together in silence, my sweaty hands sliding over the metal bench. What the hell was I doing? I wish I had the guts to just tell her to get away from Wes, but I couldn't. She pushed, and I pushed harder, each adding to this imaginary shit pile sitting between us. I wanted to break the pattern somehow because I didn't want to give her an excuse that would drive her away.

She finally broke the silence. "I got in a fight with my mom."

"A fight, huh?" I looked up at her, catching her hazel eyes in my dull browns.

She said nothing for a minute, but she was watching me intently, as if deciding if I could be trusted. "She doesn't want me to go. She told me she'd work less to be with me more, but that's all bullshit." The tension in her face subsided and the hard shell surrounding her gaze glistened as it cracked against the light coming from the street lamps off the parking lot. "She's a nurse in the city. Ever since my dad died, she's been hardcore at her job like she needs it to keep herself alive."

"May I ask," I said calmly as her eyes met mine, "how he died?"

She hesitated, biting her lower lip. "He... He got pneumonia. With his asthma, it was pretty bad."

She told me that her dad was her hero. To see the person you idolize, lying in a bed, weak and helpless, must have been heartbreaking for her. "I'm sorry."

"My mom blamed herself, said she couldn't save him. She's still trying to save him somehow, I guess." She looked back out into the field. "It hurts her too, seeing me. We always looked alike, me and my dad."

"And your brothers?"

She shrugged. "Dimitri tried and Ty... I'm not exactly close with him. They didn't understand, they still have a dad. How can they really know what it feels like?"

I watched her as she fought to keep herself from letting the memories break through her tough exterior. The colors she painted around herself were offensive and blaring, but she was no different from any other human trying to navigate through the shit life handed her. How could anyone blame a girl for building up walls, looking for anything to help her dismiss the disappointment in her life?

"And Wes?"

Ashley pivoted her head, like she was expecting an argument, but I wasn't trying to stir the pot. I wanted to understand his role in her life and why it was impossible for her to let him go.

Looking down at that same bracelet again, she pulled it slightly, raising it up her arm and back down again. "He was there. The only one it felt like. The only one who understood what I was dealing with."

Closing my eyes, I nodded softly. I got her choices, and I got why. I couldn't judge her for being stuck amid realizing the consequences of her decisions, because I was realizing my own too. The circumstances were different but it was still there, like a piece of gum on a shoe. No matter how hard you tried to scrape it off, it kept spreading and got harder to peel away. I opened my eyes to her, still lost in her reasons neatly knitted around her wrist.

"Your mom shouldn't have avoided you like that."

"Well, it's too late now. It already happened so… here we are."

The Peter Parker in me wanted to reach out and hold her, but Ashley didn't need to be protected. She needed to be understood. Keeping my gaze on her, she drifted away from me. I had to wipe that lifeless haze from her perfect face. If all I could do was distract her from what she had to face everyday of her life, then that's what I would do. For as long as she let me do it.

"You want to dance with me?"

Her head came up. "What?" she asked, eyes scrunched with bewilderment.

I slid down the bench to get beside her. "Dance with me."

A shaky smile spread across her face as she shook her head. "I don't dance."

"Everyone dances," I said, "whether it's naked in the street or alone in a closet."

"What are we going to dance to?"

I held up one of my ear buds. "I got some ideas."

I waited as her gaze darted from my hand to my face, trying to figure out what game I was playing with her.

"No one's ever asked me to dance before," she barely whispered.

"Then, you're long overdue."

Tilting her head, the corner of her lips twitched into a subtle grin. She moved toward me, touching the tip of her shoe to mine. I took her hand, and we moved out into the open field beneath the dark purple sky. Standing over her, I handed her one of my buds, which she placed slowly into her ear. It masked her natural minty scent with a creamy vanilla, which only raised the force of the blood through my veins, stomping the cruel realities I had to endure all night into dust.

I put the other ear bud in my ear and pulled out my phone, scanning the long list of tunes until falling on the one I was searching for.

Pressing play, there was a crackling silence before the sharp screech started the song's first few beats. Looking up at her, she was calm, that grin fully enveloping her rich fawn cheeks.

Putting the phone back in my pocket, I slipped my arm around her waist, holding her against me as she came mere centimeters from gracing my nose. With my other hand, I took hers, lacing our fingers together.

We moved to "Atmosphere", letting our favorite Joy Division front man, Ian Curtis, close our minds and dictate to us the sum of our lives. Resting my cheek on the side of her head, I took a step, holding her as she breathed quietly in my ear. As the song continued, she settled against the space between my neck and shoulder. I was completely lost in her, feeling her chest expand and contract against my own, the softness of her hand in mine, the scent of her hair and skin against my face. As the song winded down, we stayed locked with each other.

The next one trickled in without an ounce of resistance. Timecop1983 sent "Lovers" gently rolling into our eardrums, fueling the fluttering in my stomach and the rapid beating of my heart.

The Guardians of the Universe must have felt the pulses we radiated into the galaxy because nothing could have distracted me from her. Not the lights on the field or the rolling cars driving through the parking lot. No sound could penetrate the bubble of containment we'd created around ourselves.

As the song transitioned into the third, her hand slipped from mine to glide across my back. She squeezed me so tight; I think I lost the ability to breathe. Wrapping her in my arms, I held her against me, draping my head over her shoulder. She breathed deeply into my neck, the warmth of her breath sending my senses prickling across every inch of my skin like a ripple on the water.

I didn't know how long we were standing there. A few minutes, maybe an hour. It wasn't until Ashley pulled away with a jerk that it startled me out of my haze. Looking around, her hands fell away. I had to force myself to let her go without being too abrupt. Her eyes darted to my face as she took a step back.

"I have to go," she blurted, pulling the bud out of her ear and handing it to me.

I let it fall into my hand with no protest. She was fighting herself, scared even, of whatever was bubbling to the surface. All I could do was watch her turn back and walk off the field. There was nothing I could say that would make her stay, even though everything screamed inside me to stop her. I had to keep telling myself that we both weren't ready, me still recovering from a broken relationship and her trying to avoid one. We weren't ready; she wasn't ready… I wasn't ready.

Before she crossed through the wall of bushes leading to the parking lot, she turned to look at me, the uncertainty shuttering in her hazel eyes.

"Thanks for the dance."

"Anytime, Ashley."

A delicate smile cracked across her face before she disappeared behind the greenery. Shoving my heads in my pockets, I looked down as I listened to the crunch of her feet walking down the sidewalk, until all traces of her had abandoned my senses.

I closed my eyes and rattled the hoarseness in my throat as I exhaled into the air. The euphoria had drained from my body and I was right back where I had been before. Walking back to the bench, I released my board from my backpack, but I couldn't even plant myself on the deck for the ride home.

Who the fuck was I trying to fool? I *was* ready. She was it, the cheat code to the list of incomplete levels in my head. I fell so hard that it hurt to pick myself back up. I was in love with her, and it was real. So unimaginably real.

twenty-two

. . .

IT WAS Sunday afternoon and my shift at Grasshoppers got cut unexpectedly because Dave had a death in the family and needed to skip town for the weekend, so Logan and I had the day off to do whatever. If Dave asked me to, I would have kept the shop afloat, but he didn't give me the option. He probably didn't want to worry about it while at a funeral, especially if Logan was manning it alone for any suitable length of time.

It was crickets again with Ashley. The last text I had from her was a day or two ago.

> I got some shit to figure out. Don't be mad if u
> don't c me around too much.

> Alright. Just be safe or I'll worry about you.

> You're allowed to.

I'd be lying if I didn't think about it every day, hoping I'd see her in the hallway or that she'd be waiting by the locker room door after baseball practice. I needed dire reassurance that it wasn't a fluke, that she would not materialize like Shadow Kat right through me.

It didn't help that Chris's confession still lingered in the back of my mind. He was incredibly careful around me, like I'd bring out the adamantium claws and start slashing throats Wolverine style. I mean… whatever. I cared a little, probably more than I would like to admit, but Chris was one of my best friends and Mari was my first. If they ever started dating, it would be weird, sure, but I'd get over it. It wasn't worth losing Chris over. We only had a few months of school left. Work and vacations consumed summer before adulthood officially began. Any time I had with these guys wouldn't go to waste.

"You got this," Logan sat on one of the many half walls of the mall parking lot.

I was attempting to perform a few simple heel flips on my board. Compared to me, Logan was a much more advanced trick boarder than I was. I was more of a cruiser, enjoying going down steep hills in the middle of an empty street, the wind against my face with my earbuds glued in. Aside from comic books and baseball, boarding was something that fit nicely in my personality glove, but not nearly as high of a priority as it was for Logan. I'd be lying if I said Logan wasn't lazy, but when it was something he was really passionate about, he gave it his all.

This was my fourth attempt at getting this down. I could get the board up, sure, but twisting it was giving me trouble. It was like a flick of the wrist, Logan had told me, only with your feet. Easier said than done, as everything in life was. I only kicked it or turned it over belly up. Getting it back around was the hard part.

"Slide your foot around it, like those fancy folks do with wine glasses."

After another failed flip, landing me on the bottom of my board, I looked up at him. "What exactly do fancy folk do with their wine glasses, Logan?"

"You know." He held out his hand, touching his thumb to the rest of his digits, making a circle. Taking his other hand, he ran his index finger around the top with a rather alluring smile. "Fingering the rim."

"Wow." I raised my eyebrows with a smirk. "That's an attractive way to look at it."

We both burst out laughing at the thought. I mean, we are guys after all. Shit like this is always funny.

"Hey, I forgot to tell you," Logan added after recovering from our fit of laughter, "I set sail for the new X-Games establishment in August."

"No shit! That's awesome, dude!"

"Land of the rising sun, here I come!"

"Uh, that's Japan."

He shrugged. "Well, California is closer. I could hop on a plane and be there in a day!"

"If you ever go to Japan without me, I will skin you alive."

"Can't make any promises," he said, "gives you a reason to visit me once I'm there."

"I don't need a reason, but going to Japan is an added incentive."

Logan jumped down from the wall. "Maybe come with? You still up in the air on what you're doing after we graduate?"

Picking up my board, I flipped it once or twice in my hands. "I'm pretty far gone with that, lost in space practically."

"Don't worry about it. You'll know it when it hits you."

That was the problem. It hit me; it hit me like a train going a thousand miles an hour. I just didn't know if I realized it too late.

We didn't skateboard too much longer after that. It was nice to just do guy things and take my mind off how anxious I was about Ashley. Not seeing or hearing from her the last few days left my stomach inflated like a balloon, just floating and taking up internal space. I must have checked my phone an unnatural amount of times every night, seeing if I missed a call or a text from her, but there was always nothing.

We walked through the parking lot with the mall on our left. The fastest way out of here was by hopping a fence onto Myers Avenue to make it into my neck of the Hicksville woods. The day was still young, and we had a lot of video games and pizza planned for the evening. Chris was going to swing by later too, and maybe Tom.

Pulling out my phone, I clicked on the screen, but only the battle ridden image of Spider-Man and the Green Goblin graced my lock screen. Still no texts or calls from Ashley. I siphoned through my contacts and tapped her number to send her a message.

> Hey. Just checkin in. Hope ur okay.

"When do you think Dave is going to give us a heads up on inventory?" Logan's question pulled me out of my anxiety.

"I have no clue." I shoved my phone back in my pocket. "But I bet it will be the day before it happens."

"Day of, more than likely."

We were about a mall block away from the Myers Ave. divider when a loud, panicked scream came from out of nowhere. Someone ran out from one of the alleys, a girl with long dark hair and white sneakers. I didn't need an introduction to know it was Amber. A few bangs and scraping metal on the blacktop brought Logan and me to a stop. Amber grabbed out her phone before looking in our direction. A flash of relief widened her eyes as she came sprinting toward us.

"Pete," she choked as she tried to catch her breath, "Wes is... with Ashley..."

"What?" Looking up the street and back down again, I remembered that this was the same strip Ashley had taken me to where those alley cats lived.

Amber grabbed my arm, shaking me. "Stop him, Pete!"

She didn't need to tell me twice; I was already making a beeline toward all the screaming and heavy arguing that was radiating from the alley.

"Pete!" Logan yelled.

"Get mall security or 911!" I shouted. I didn't even glance back at him to see if he was following me. I just wanted to get to where Ashley was. If he laid a hand on her... goddammit, where was a radioactive spider when you needed one?

I turned the corner of the alley as my eyes fell on them. Wes was there, his hair slicked back with a few loose strands hanging in his wildly upturned face. In his hand, he clutched one of the small meowing kittens, who was wriggling and scratching at his thick fingers as it desperately tried to get away. Ashley was hanging on his arm, pulling and begging him to let go of the tiny creature. There was no mother in sight or any sign of the other ones.

"Let him go, Wes!" she shouted, reaching up toward the finger tethered ball of fur.

"Why should I?" he mocked, his arm not even phased by the weight of her. With his other hand, he pushed her back against the wall with a thud.

"You're a fucking liar!" he growled at her. "You think you can dance around me? You think you're so slick, don't you?"

His back was to me, my only chance to do anything. To act as any self-respecting, love-struck teenager would when they saw the girl they had fallen for being pushed around by some arrogant hot headed asshole.

Running at top speed, I jumped on Wes's back, locking my arms around his neck and squeezing as hard as I could. He dropped the kitten and stumbled on his feet. The kitten made a mad dash under the dumpsters, but Wes was too much of a seasoned brawler to let my scrawny ass shake him, even if he wasn't expecting it. Okay, scrawny is the wrong word, but compared to his bulging muscles and megaladon stature, I had little a chance.

My feet barely touched the ground as he stumbled around with me on his back, his hands grabbing my arms, trying to pry me off. Unstable staggering finally pushed us back, and he resolved to slamming me into the painted brick wall to see if that would dislodge me.

When he did it a second time, it was a lot harder and shook my brain around in my skull. He pried my arms off before sending me flying over his shoulder with a back body drop. Or an over the shoulder arm drag. It must have dislodged my glasses because when my lungs were able to work again and I could finally open my eyes, fuzziness clouded my vision.

"Look who we have… *here*!" His foot met my stomach, the tip of his boots rattling my ribcage and stifling my gasps for air. I rolled over on my hands and knees, trying desperately to get up so I could at least attempt to defend myself. Ashley crouched down next to me, grabbing my arm and yanking me like a puppet on a string. "Get up!" she said, glaring at Wes as she tried to drag me away from him.

"Don't fucking touch him!" she yelled, her voice loud and aggressive, like the way she sounded when I first stepped in between them that night on the street. She sounded like herself again, but that wasn't necessarily a good thing, at least for keeping Wes from blowing his shit.

"How many times have you fucked this loser, huh?" Wes said, stepping toward us like Mike Tyson on a good day.

He grabbed her by the shirt, yanking her up to his face. Even though I was wobbly on my legs, I kept hold of Ashley's arm. With all the control I could muster, I slammed my forehead into Wes' face, knocking him backward as I pulled Ashley against me. If my head wasn't spinning before, it was on a tilt-a-whirl malfunction now.

"Goddammit!" I cringed, bringing my hand up to press against the throbbing pain between my glassless eyes.

Soft, shaking hands met my face, "You're bleeding." I could barely make out her face, but she was there in front of me, her mouth turned, eyes alert.

"I can't see anything." I tried not to sound panicked, letting the adrenaline kick my flight response to the curb. I could hear Wes reeling behind her, his hands cupping his nose as blood dripped from the cracks between his fingers. If he wasn't at his breaking point already, he sure as hell was now.

"You motherfucker!" he shouted.

He was coming at us again, Ashley too distracted to notice the blur of his fist sailing toward the back of her head. "Watch out!"

Pushing her away, his punch landed across my sacrificial face. I didn't know if I spun around on my feet or if that was just the fluid in my skull switching on the spin cycle, but the next thing I knew, I was on the ground, lying on the unclean blacktop of the alley, staring at beat up green dumpsters and muffled feet coming in and out of focus. The four feet soon became six, then eight, and that was when I couldn't keep my eyes open anymore and the sounds of silence crept in.

twenty-three

. . .

"I'M SORRY, Pete! I'm sorry!"

Muffled, weak, but it was her. The sound of Ashley's voice forced the pain briefly from my eyes. I couldn't focus correctly, but I tried to find her. "Ashley?"

As my eyelids broke the wall of darkness it had plunged me into, I saw an unfamiliar face hovering above me. A woman in a blue uniform with her brown hair pulled back was all I could really make out. The bright light shining in my face smudged the rest of her features.

"Kid, can you hear me?"

A flash of red donned her shoulder, so I assumed she was an EMT. With a dull drag of my arm, I tried to shield myself to keep the blinding beam from burning my corneas. "Yeah, yeah…"

Coming back to consciousness sucked big time. A throbbing pain radiated inside my brain from one ear to the other. It was like an alien was trying to burst out of my skull and leave the contents of my noodle contorted brain splayed out all over my lifeless body. I tried to sit up, but the woman's hand came to rest on my shoulder. "Just try to relax, we're taking you to the hospital."

As she moved away, I got a better picture of my surroundings. I was in an ambulance all right. The shiny silver walls were undeniable. Glancing to my side, I saw the curved metal bars of the gurney I was resting on. "Where's Ashley?"

"Pete!" Logan's voice sprang loose as he came into view. Turning my head was like turning the knob on a rusted over water socket. I made out his wavy surfer hair, even though dark spots still danced in my field of vision. Amber was with him, sitting with her arms wrapped around her knees. She looked up at me when I turned and moved over to the stretcher.

"Your parents will meet us at the hospital," the EMT said. "You got pretty banged up, but you'll be fine."

"Where's Ashley?"

"Dude, that was the most epic thing I have ever seen in my life!" Logan was beaming with furious energy, like coming out of a John Wick 3 viewing. It was a little too much for me right now, especially since I just got my ass kicked by the most wanted douche bag in town.

"Where–"

"She went home." Amber's voice joined the fray. "You were out for a while. Her mom came and got her. She wanted to stay."

"And Wes?"

Adding to his already unmeasurable glee, Logan's smile spread as far as it could stretch. "Arrested man! Fucking arrested! Taken away in a cop car and everything."

"He really messed you up, Pete," Amber hissed, like she didn't already know.

"Mission accomplished." I brought myself up on my elbows. The door to the back of the ambulance was wide open. Two cop cars and one of the mall security golf carts, or whatever they wanted to call them, were still sitting with their lights flashing. A few witnesses were talking to the police.

Logan shook his head. "You really have a death wish, don't you?"

His comment radiated unneeded heat into my already throbbing brain, not something I needed to be experiencing. "I don't give a shit. It wasn't about me so, fuck you."

"Hey, I get it. Lois Lane part two! You're amazing, man."

Amber's lips went thin and her eyes reserved. "Well, I'm glad you'll be okay." She slipped off the metal floor of the ambulance and jumped down to the ground, disappearing behind the left-side corner.

"Here, I found these." Logan handed me my glasses, battered and missing an arm.

"Thanks."

"So," he said with a sigh, "I guess no gaming tonight, huh?"

"Wow Logan, thanks for your undeniable concern."

The hospital revealed I suffered a minor concussion and bruising to my ribs. My nose and jaw were miraculously unbroken, but that didn't stop my face from swelling up like a balloon. I got to stay home for the rest of the week. Every day I wasn't in school, my phone exploded with texts from random people commending me on both my stupidity and bravery. Apparently, this was far too big for Logan to contain all to himself.

He spread the story of my heroics to everyone who was within earshot, and it spread like wildfire, even to Kim's campus. I took the infamous Westley De La Cruz down. A glasses wearing baseball player who works at a comic book store, who'd have thunk? My parents weren't as thrilled about it as everyone else. They couldn't really punish me. I think getting my ass kicked was punishment enough.

Believe me, I was seriously glad I was not in school when this story first dropped. It would have been impossible to avoid anyone. At least with hearing it from outside sources or buzzing on my phone, I could just tune it out. I didn't want to think about it because I hadn't heard from or of Ashley. Not at all. After a few days of not being able to even look at anything electronic, I sent her a text, but no reply. I tried every day since, but she was completely ignoring me.

Even when I asked Logan or Chris if they'd seen her, they always said no. Apparently, she hadn't been at school either.

"Not even Amber?" I asked when Chris, Tom, and Logan came by to hang out about three days after the incident.

"I talked to Amber," Logan told me. "Ashley is out, something to do with Wes getting arrested."

I remember when she said that her mom didn't even know she was seeing Wes. That could not have gone over well, having to pick her up and seeing Wes getting dragged into a police car. Not the highlight of any parents' day. The legality of it. Maybe she was in trouble or getting accused of something by that asshole. I could totally see Wes throwing Ashley under the bus for some bullshit that he had done, trying to save his own skin.

Fucking low life.

Friday came, and I spent most of the day lying on my bed, doing some school work that they sent home to me, just to keep myself from worrying about her. Mari brought it over this time, which kind of surprised me. She stayed a bit, telling me about this and that, but even she couldn't distract me enough. Trying to ignore my phone buzzing was impossible because every time I looked at it, I hoped it was Ashley.

At the kitchen table, I barely touched my bag of crispy, delicious Doritos and half-assed Ham and Swiss sandwich. My head was... better, but not great. It still mildly hurt when I made any sudden movements, but mostly, I was on my feet. Half of it was worrying and half was me going stir crazy. I was not someone you would call antisocial. I like to think that I am, but really, I wasn't. Being in school, on the baseball team, hanging out with my friends, and working are part of my existence, and it had never been this disrupted before. I was lucky if I got two sick days a year during school. This was the last year, and I was missing more than I wanted to.

My phone buzzed against the wooden table. Picking it up seemed like a waste of time, but I did, and immediately my heart jumped when I saw Ashley's name flash across the screen. I couldn't press accept fast enough as I fumbled the phone to my ear.

"Hey." Her voice woke me up. She didn't sound like her usual self, but she didn't sound totally upset, either.

"Hey. How are you doing?"

"I'm... hanging in there," she said cautiously.

"That bad, huh?"

"Could be worse." There was a sharp enthusiasm in her voice that time, more like the Ashley I knew, followed by a few seconds of silence. "I'm sorry I didn't call sooner. My mom took my phone away."

"That's okay. I'm glad you called."

There were a few long seconds of silence as I tried to find words that would make sense in this conversation, but she beat me to it. "How are you?"

"Still in one piece." I sat up in my chair. "I wanted to ask you–"

"We need to stop."

A jolt of uneasiness shot to my stomach. "Stop what?"

"Stop… whatever it is we're doing."

Closing my eyes, I locked my tongue behind my pressed lips. "Why?"

"I just… there's a lot of shit going on right now."

She didn't have to remind me of that, being in the aftermath of said shit. It sounded like she was just trying to make excuses, but I couldn't jump down her throat for it.

She sighed into the phone. "I shouldn't have dragged you into all this. You got hurt because of me and my fucking bullshit. I should have just left you alone. I'm sorry."

Her voice carried like a plea, validating that she was stringing me along the entire time, making sure she tied the knot every time. I tried to keep the shaken nerves from leaking through my voice. I needed to be honest now.

"If you told me that last month, I'd probably agree with you, but I don't regret anything."

"Do you have brain damage?"

"Well, technically I do, but that's not the point."

Doing this over the phone pried my already bruised ribs apart. I wasn't sure how to control myself. It was like watching those videos on YouTube, the ones of soldiers coming home after being gone for months on end. And their dog saw them from the window, their tails wagging like helicopter blades, their bodies bursting with so much excitement they couldn't stand still? I was the dog, ready to jump through a window to get to her, but I couldn't because I lacked the ability to make it happen.

"You pulled me out of this funk. I don't know this… Dr. Strange time stone loop that made everything feel hopeless, like no matter what I did, it wouldn't be the right thing to do."

"And how did I do that?"

"Just… being you."

She said nothing after that, letting my confession sink in, I guess. There was so much more I wanted to say, but I didn't want to sound desperate, even though all I could think about was being with her.

"Can I see you?"

"I… don't think you should."

"There's more I want to say–"

"Weren't you listening to anything I said? We can't anymore, Pete. This has to be over. I'm done, okay? Don't make it harder than it has to be."

My heart was beating at a frantic pace, raising the hairs on my arms. "If you just need some space to clear your head, that's totally cool–"

"I don't want to." Her voice wavered to keep herself grounded. She was barely holding it together.

"So," I said through rattled teeth, "you're just going to avoid me?"

"There's only a few months of school left. You never noticed me before, so it shouldn't be too hard to not notice me now."

"You think you're that easy to forget about?"

"Please, Pete, I'm asking you to just do this… for me?" Her words held me hostage against the plea.

Closing my eyes, I tried to think of something else to say to convince her this was a bad idea, but nothing was going to change her mind. She already decided this long before she made this phone call. Maybe she was thinking about it for days and was just too afraid to do it, making sure all her I's were dotted and her T's crossed so she wouldn't fall apart.

"Fine," I forced out. "If that's what you want."

"This isn't easy for me, you just don't understand."

"No, I do, I understand."

Did I really? I knew she was stubborn and wouldn't change her mind. Her mom was probably pissed beyond reason. I was sure the police had talked to Ashley a few times already regarding Wes and his laundry list of felonies, but to do it all alone? They only grabbed me once at the hospital and it was torture answering their endless questions with a throbbing headache, but once was bad enough. As much as I wanted to be there, she was denying me that, even as a friend. The stinging in my stomach only got worse. She didn't want to be saved this time, that much I understood.

"I'm glad you're doing okay." She finally said.

"Yeah."

"Don't jump in front of anymore fists."

"Sure."

Another hesitation, another moment to reach again, but neither of us did.

"Bye then." She finally said.

I waited, hoping she would just hang up, but she didn't. She was waiting for me to say it too. "Bye."

Clicking end call was ending a lot more than that. I stared at the slowly rotating ceiling fan above the table, focusing on one blade as it circled the lights over and over repeatedly. I wasn't angry. I wasn't sad. I was… defeated. The ache in my ribs spread throughout my entire body, digging a well for all the pain and misery to hide and collect until it spilled over. There were so many times I had tried to get away from her, avoid her at all costs. Now all I wanted was for her to be there and she wasn't… she wouldn't be.

"Hey." Kim crossed the doorway to the kitchen. "You look like shit."

I gave a meek grin. "Thanks."

"What's bugging you?" She sat down, leaning her head into her hand.

"Just… stuff…"

There was no way I could describe this unusual cross between being physically wounded and emotionally crushed. My face, my hands, legs, everything seemed big and awkward. Nothing was being stimulated or tested or answered. I didn't care that people were ranting and raving about what I'd done, because it didn't matter. It wasn't the aftermath or even the actions I took to stop Wes. It was the fact that I never cared less about my well-being than at that moment.

This couldn't be a normal feeling that people go through or, if it was, no one dared talk about what it took to get there.

"Do you need a break?"

Rolling my eyes up to meet hers, I couldn't even remember what I was looking at before hearing her voice again. Nodding was about all I could do. Clearly, I had never looked so pathetic to her in my entire life.

"Where do you want to go?"

"The mall..."

She leaned back. "You sure?"

"Yeah. I'm sure."

After we got into the car, the drive over there was all a blur. The coldness of the window as I leaned my forehead against it was about the only sensation I was allowing myself to experience. When we pulled into the mall parking lot, I forced my head up.

"The alley," I pointed, "can we drive by there?"

"Where it happened?" Kim asked. "If that's where you want to go."

I liked that she didn't ask me why like she usually would; she seemed to understand that I needed some closure or a sense of realism regarding the whole thing. Frankly, I didn't really understand why I wanted to go back there. My internal compass was just forcing the needle in that direction.

She pulled over to the side of the mall, right in front of the alley where my heroics were witnessed and manifested into some sort of high school legend. Treading out of the car, the hardened blacktop seemed unnaturally familiar, like it knew me far too well. I took a few steps into the depths of the crack between the buildings. There wasn't police tape or even a hint of what happened five days ago. No one would have ever known what went down here just by looking at it, already forgotten, lost to the passing of time.

"You okay?" Kim was standing next to me. I hadn't even realized she had gotten out of the car.

"I don't know."

We were quiet for a while, just standing in the alley like we were waiting for something to happen, or at least, I was. I couldn't understand why this wasn't solving anything for me. I thought coming here would lift the boulders off me and allow me to see how all these pieces that had fallen out of alignment would fit together.

This wasn't a fucking comic book to me and I wasn't the unexpected hero. I was just a kid– just a kid who hadn't recognized how much that four letter word could really just shake everything loose so easily.

This place would do nothing for me. At least I tried, "We can get out of here," I said with a long, breathy sigh.

"Sure."

Glancing at her, I managed a weak smile. "Thanks for taking me."

She put her hand around my shoulders. "You know I'm here for you."

A tiny noise, almost like a squeak, stumbled from under one of the dumpsters. A furry little kitten ran out into the alley. It looked up with its yellow eyes and came meowing over to where we stood. Bending down, I picked up the furry little creature and held it in my hands. It was the one Wes had been holding when I first jumped him. He was skinny, like he hadn't eaten in a few days. I didn't see any sign of the rest of them. He was alone, maybe the only one left.

"Look at that little guy!" Kim squealed, tickling the little fur ball behind the ears.

The little motor inside his chest rumbled in an over expulsion of loving purrs. I immediately took in his warmth, this little ball of love tingling away the numbness in my fingers and lifting it from my bones.

Kim continued to rub the top of his head with her finger. "He looks hungry, poor thing."

"I'm not going to college," I blurted out.

Looking at me, Kim grinned with silent victory. "Good."

"I'll tell Mom and Dad when they get home."

"About time you said something." She looked back at the little furry creature in my hands. "What are you going to do with that guy?"

"His name is Gremlin," I said. "And we're taking him home with us."

"Totally agree."

She motioned toward the car. "Let's get to it then. We'll swing by the pet store and get some stuff."

I followed her to the car, slid into my seat and shut the door. Gremlin curled up and started licking my fingers. He smelled terrible, and I could see little fleas crawling through his fur. The purring never stopped. He was just glad someone had come for him, that he wasn't alone anymore and would probably stuff his face with cat food soon. A little creature, whose life had been so unpredictable and probably unfair, was still just so ready to be loved and give love.

"I should have told her." The words just fell from my mouth like unexpected rain.

"Told her what?"

"That I've fallen in love with her."

She nodded. "You should have. That shit doesn't wait for anyone."

Sinking into the back of the seat, I brought Gremlin to my chest, letting him dig his little claws into my shirt. "It's too late now."

"Who says?"

"She ended it, before it could even start."

"Before it could start? What are you, a moron? It already started."

Lifting my head up, I glanced at Kim as we drove. "It doesn't matter if it did or didn't."

She shook her head, her mouth hung open. "Why are you giving up?"

"I'm not."

"Yeah, you are!"

"Well, what the hell can I do?"

Coming up to a stoplight, Kim sighed and settled back in her seat. "She's in a world of shit now. She obviously wants to deal with it on her own, so I say let her. She'll let you know when she's ready."

"How do you know that?"

"Girls are tricky, but you'll know. As long as you keep your eyes and ears open."

That got an enthusiastic scoff out of me. "What am I, a fucking hound dog?"

"Hawk Eye," she said, rolling her eyes at me. "There, is that a better comparison for you?"

"I guess so."

The car started moving again as we merged into a left turning lane. "Stop feeling sorry for yourself. If she feels the same about you," Kim looked at me, "she'll come through."

"What if she doesn't?"

"Then she's more of an idiot than I thought."

"She's not an idiot."

"Then you have nothing to worry about."

The car turned left as smooth as a left turn could go. Hanging on to Gremlin so he didn't squirm off my chest, I tickled my finger under his chin. His body rumbled with ten times the ferocity and his eyes closed in comforting cuteness. "It's not that easy."

"News flash, life sucks sometimes." We went over a bump, and Kim slowed down as we turned into the pet store parking lot. "You spend all your time looking down at your feet. Eventually, your neck will hurt so much you will have to look up. When you do, you'll see all the goddamn beautiful things you've missed and hate yourself for it."

After making a right, we pulled into a parking spot. She rolled into a spot and pulled up the window before turning to face me. "I don't think you want to miss this one rare and beautiful thing, do you?"

Fuck her. Why did she have to read between the lines on everything? I swear she was some sort of witch doctor.

"Stop being right all the time."

She smiled as she opened the door. "Impossible."

I stepped out of the car, holding Gremlin against my chest. "How long do I wait?"

"You'll know. Or I'll make you. Whichever comes first."

Looking down at the kitten in my arms, I couldn't help but smile at his adorable fuzziness. Even if Ashley says no and we went our separate ways, I swore an oath. The leader of the keeper of the kittens would want to know this little guy was okay.

twenty-four

. . .

IT WAS A NICE MAY MORNING/AFTERNOON, and the senior class at Hicksville high school made their way out onto the football field to be released, officially, into the world. We were a sea of caps, gowns, and orange tassels as every parent, sibling and relative watching crossed their fingers and hoped for the best.

Telling my folks I wasn't planning on going to college did not surprise them, but they were a little disappointed in me, especially Dad. Letting me keep Gremlin was a walk in the park by comparison.

"I wish you would," Dad told me, "but I respect your decision to wait."

"What will you do in the meantime?" Mom asked.

That was the big question, a question I wasn't sure of the answer because I wasn't sure what was going to happen.

Sitting in our designated chairs, I watched as the first half of the graduating class made their way to the stage. My face broke into an enormous smile once I saw Ashley walk up to grab her diploma. Her hair was in its usual state, billowing out from underneath her cap.

I did what she asked; I kept my distance from her for the rest of the school year. We passed each other in the halls sometimes. I would smile and she'd wave at me. A few times, I shot her a text about anything other than us. She wouldn't blow me off, but the conversations never lasted long. I'd take what I could get. She didn't completely drop me. That had to mean something.

Baseball came and went. We didn't make the playoffs this year, but it was still a pretty fun ride. Tom slowly became a regular buddy of ours at the lunch table and on our weekend hangouts, probably because he got the balls to ask Rina out. They were a couple now, as much as Rina was shy to admit it. It would probably be a miracle seeing them do anything together but blush and hold hands. It was cute, and that was coming from a guy. Maybe the message sank in. It was now or never.

Rina got one of the top academic scholarships anyone could hope to achieve, if you could call Valedictorian a high honor, that is. No, she deserved it. Chris got his baseball scholarship and Mari got into Juilliard. It shocked me she planned to pursue it too, something that wasn't a simple decision for her dad to accept. But she was good and it took a successful tryout to one of the top arts schools in the country for his eyes open.

After the ceremony, we tossed our caps into the air as the last nail on the high school head. Parents and family members poured onto the field to congratulate whoever they came to see. My parents and Kim came down, gave me the 'I'm-proud-of-you' hug and took a bunch of pictures. As mom and dad went to congratulate some of their fellow parents for successfully getting their kids through high school, I spied Amber talking to her parents.

"You did it! I can't believe it."

Kim gave me a hug, squeezing me tight. Barely able to get my arms around her, I huffed as the air leaked out of my lungs slower and slower. "Take it easy!"

"I'm sorry, I'm sorry. I just–" She pulled away with her lips pouting. "You're just so grown up now! Short stack no more!"

"Wow, you're funny."

She pushed me and smiled. "You're lucky."

"Why is that?"

"Because you're in the clear. There is nothing holding you back anymore. How does it feel?"

"I don't know." I shrugged. "I guess I haven't found out yet."

Chris came over to us and patted me on the back, grabbing my shoulders and squeezing me excitedly. "We did it, man!"

"Yeah, congratulations." I said.

"Hey, Kim," Chris waved, "how's it going?"

"Hey, Chris, congrats on that scholarship, you deserve it."

"Thanks."

Behind me, Kim patted me on the back. "I'll catch you at the car. Let me know if you see Ashley so you can give her that thing."

"Yeah, I'll see ya."

She walked across the field toward the parking lot. Chris watched her go before looking back at me with his eyes squinting in confusion. "What thing would that be?"

"It's… nevermind."

"I don't want to know, anyway." He gave a long-winded sigh, a decompression from the excitement or exhaustion, or maybe it was both. "So, grabbing the science award, that's awesome, man! Just like Peter Parker."

"I wouldn't have it any other way."

We laughed as he pulled away from me. "After all that worrying about graduating, how do you feel? Honestly."

"I don't know." I shrugged. "I guess I'm a little relieved."

"Yo," Logan lumbered up to us, hands outstretched, "our day has come, gentleman!"

"It sure has." Chris brought Logan in for a bro hug.

"So, where's the party tonight? I heard Dante is throwing a basher!"

"Wouldn't you rather just chill out with some good ol' fashion pizza, munchies, and video games?" I asked.

"No fucking way. This is our moment! We got to go out with a bang! Let loose a little."

"I don't know…" I said jokingly.

"What are you boys up to?"

Mari, Rina and Tom came over to us, each wearing their own version of an ear to ear grin.

"Congratulations, guys." Tom made a round of shoulder slaps for each of us.

"Thanks, man. You too. We're off to the bases!" Chris boasted.

"Brown University, here we come!"

They clasped hands all Predator-esque, only without the jacked muscles, and brought it in for a cross body bump.

"You better come and visit me." Rina raised her eyebrows at Tom.

"Yeah, yeah… I mean, of course. Boston isn't that far from Rhode Island."

"Every weekend."

Gulping, Tom's nerves were getting the better of him. A joke, or so he didn't think, but a gingerly nudge from Mari sent both the girls into a joint giggle at his expense.

"She's just kidding, Tom, calm down."

"Oh yeah, right?" Tom shifted nervously.

I gave Tom a reassuring pat on the back. "Mari is rubbing off on her, you'd better watch out."

Mari looked at me and laughed. "Ha ha. You're funny."

That look that pinned me back when I was a sophomore slid across her face. The right corner of her lip coming up ever so much, and her long, dark hair falling to one side. For a second, it took me back to that feeling of when I first realized I liked her more than a friend. But I remembered that the person who I was back then was not the person I had become. So much has changed in such a short amount of time. It was crazy how much your life can just completely turn around, especially when you're lost and afraid.

"So what's the plan? Head on over to the burger joint, then hit up the party?" Logan asked.

"What are you, from the 50s?" I chuckled, rubbing the back of my neck. "I'll meet up with you guys. There's something I have to do first."

Chris smiled and dropped his hand on my shoulder again. "Sure thing, man."

"Yeah, I'll text you when I'm coming."

"All right, cool."

I patted Chris on the back and raised my hand to Logan, who took it with a reassuring grasp. "Catch you later."

"We'll see you, Pete." Rina said with a smile.

"See ya," I said as I moved away from my anchors, the friends I never planned to lose. They didn't have a choice, and neither did I.

I broke out into a light jog as I caught up to Amber, who was slipping away from the crowd with her folks. "Amber!"

She turned, a meager expression on her face. "Peter."

Glancing back at her parents, she smiled at me, but I could tell it was a trial attempt. "Congrats on the science award."

"Yeah, thanks. And you, I heard you're taking cheerleading all the way to Minnesota."

She shrugged, holding in the obvious excitement she was not ready to share with anyone, least of all me. "Not just for cheerleading. Psychology mostly."

"Nice. I feel you'd be good at that."

She cracked a grin, "I think so."

"Listen, um… I wanted to ask you–"

"She's doing okay," Amber reassured me. "Got a restraining order on Westley, believe it or not."

"Wow, uh… I wasn't expecting that."

"She wised up to him finally, a little late but better than never, right?"

"Right."

I hesitated to ask her for any more information. Amber sighed, looking away before taking a step toward me. "It's been tough on her, the whole thing, but she needed to figure this out on her own."

Nodding my head, I looked down at my well-dressed feet, the black polish of my shoes digging into the pure green grass of the field. It was hard to hear. I mean, I didn't think she needed me or anyone, but… I wanted to be more than just a way out. Believing it was hard, and I didn't want to. I didn't think I had to because I sensed it wasn't the truth. But maybe it was.

"I was hoping to talk to her, but I haven't–"

"She's parked over by the baseball field."

My head shot up to Amber's crossed arms and half smirking eyes. "Well? What are you waiting for? Don't you have somewhere to be?"

twenty-five

. . .

ASHLEY WAS SITTING on the hood of her car, her cap dangling between raised knees from her fingers, skimming through an open comic book. There was no one else around, the perfect hiding spot away from all the commotion and celebration just across the lot. For a second, she didn't notice me standing there, too lost in the colorful pages of heroism and hope.

"Hey," I announced.

With a slight turn of her head, her eyes fell on me, bright and expressionless, "Oh, hey."

I made my way to the car, keeping my hands behind my back and trying not to let Gremlin slip. "*Skydoll*, huh?"

"Yeah," she flipped the comic closed and placed it on the car. "It's good stuff."

"I got you something."

Without fumbling too much, I pulled my arms around, placing the now three or four-month-old fuzzball Gremlin had become. He seemed unsure about the surface of the car and walked around in a circle on his little cat toes before falling over on his side with a thump.

"Holy shit, Pete!" Ashley's face lit up as she scooped him into her hands, touching her nose to his little whiskers and enjoying the gentle rumbling of his instant purrs.

"I went back, after everything happened," leaned against the car. "He was there, alone, so I hope you don't mind that I adopted one of your cats."

"And you didn't say anything?" Looking back at me with eyes half giving way to tears, she took in a swell of air and let out a sigh. "What's his name?"

"Gremlin."

"Of course," she smirked, looking at the kitten again. "It suits him."

I let her bask in kitten glory for a bit. It was relieving to see her so happy with that little wiggly insta-purr in her hands. If that was the only thing I could give her, I would be content to leave it that way.

"So," she looked at me, letting her hands fall to the car so Gremlin could escape onto her lap. "I heard they offered you that baseball scholarship."

I leaned against the car, raising an eyebrow and trying to hide my smile as I shook my head. "You heard that?"

"Yeah, word gets around."

"I didn't take it. Did that get around too?"

"Yeah." She stared at me for a while, studying me almost. "Why didn't you?"

She was waiting for something to fall, expecting it almost. Sitting cross-legged on her car as Gremlin made a jungle gym out of her lap, the wind kissed her face and played with her kinky crown. I wish it was easy to be bold, because if I was, I wouldn't wait for her permission. I would kiss her right now. But unlike Wes, I wanted her to have a choice, even though resisting the pull to run my fingers through her hair and feel her skin was splitting me in two.

"Someone else deserved it."

Her legs slid down against the hood as she looked back down at Gremlin. "How did that go over with your folks?"

"They don't really have a choice."

Her eyes closed softly before opening wide again. "Wow, finally stepping up, Pete."

We smiled at each other in the same millisecond. I took a deep breath, making sure I was looking at her and not where my nerves were telling me to avoid.

"I think a year off will do me some good."

She narrowed her eyes at me. "You sure about that?"

"I don't know," I shrugged, "but I'm okay with it. The whole not knowing thing it's… it's exciting."

"Dropping all the weight, ready to take on the world now? Shit, Pete, what happened?"

If I had any ounce of singing ability, I would belt out a ballad in how much she had shifted my life in the most disruptive and freeing way possible, but luckily for her, I was a terrible singer. "Well, what about you? I heard about the restraining order against Wes. Should I get one too?"

She lowered her arms beside her, tossing herself onto her stomach to face me, resting her face in her palms. She was a few inches from me, maybe a foot. The immediate scent of her carried in the wind, whipping my pulse into high gear. Raising an eyebrow at me, she pulled at one of her spiral locks, twirling it in her fingers with a tempting grin. Gremlin continued to crawl in between her elbows and under her chest, with no protest from her. "Yeah, you should."

"Sounds like you want me to."

"Maybe."

Her eyes trailed to Gremlin, who was rubbing against her vigorously. Waiting there with her, we remained silent as the distant conversations across the way were fading to the sounds of car doors shutting and engines peeling out of their parking spaces. She bit the corner of her lip, flashing a shy glance at me.

It was happening again, that prickly feeling of my hair standing up against the smooth customary gown, the beating in my chest growing louder and louder with each passing second of uncertainty. The balloon in my stomach, swelled to an unimaginable girth, on the verge of bursting. It was now or never, and I wasn't ready for never. I was ready for now.

"I'm sorry," she shifting her weight from one elbow to the other, "for shutting you out."

I shrugged. "You did what you had to do."

She looked down at her naked arm, the bracelet that once decorated her wrist now gone. "You don't hate me for it?"

"Nah." I shifted my feet and shook my head. "I don't think I could hate you."

Her nerves broke with a smile as her arms fell in front of her. She leaned toward the windshield, tilting her head tohover above her shoulder. "Are you sure about that? Cause I swear I've seen you hate me."

"You thought that was hate? That was just me being a dick. I can be a dick, sure. That's what you probably saw." Her smile only grew at that, breaking into the realm of the most beautiful. It was hard to stray away, even though you'd have to be Riddler level mad to even think of missing a single instant of her.

"I was afraid you'd forget about me." Her chin fell to her chest rather meekly.

"That's… impossible."

"Why?" She shifted in front of me again, coming up on her knees, creating a fragile distance from me. "Did you do something stupid and fall in love with me or something?"

She was trying to play it off as a joke, but there was a shred of hopefulness in her voice. The way she shifted and sat back up, like an anxious kid who was about to confess that the biggest tattle of their life was a lie. Those three words I've wanted to say to her since that day coming out of homeroom. So even though I could feel my knees buckling and my sweaty hands glide against the tan surface of the car, I had to do it. If nothing would change from it, at least I knew I held nothing back.

"Yeah," I admitted, holding my breath. "I did… fall in love with you."

She stared at me, searching for some sign that I was fucking with her, just being a guy, saying what I thought she wanted to hear. There wasn't a single doubt in my mind. No devil on my shoulder pulling at my conscience, telling me I was bullshitting myself. This was real.

The silence was crawling into my ears like angry ants. I didn't know what she was thinking, if she felt relief or nausea. I had to break the silence before the balloon stretched anymore than it already had.

"So," I swallowed the lump of doubt sitting in my throat, "now you know." I pushed off of the car, wiping my palms across my gown, "Do you still want me to leave you alone forever?"

Her eyes caught the light of the afternoon sun, that curved grin I could not get enough of, making its way across her face again. "I don't want you to leave me alone, I never did."

I slid my hand across the hood of the car, lacing my fingers through the cracks of her own. She didn't resist but held on to me with an immediate purpose, her soft skin sending sparks up my arm to jump start the beating of my heart. Gremlin continued his love onslaught of face rubbing and unprecedented purring, sending vibrations between our fingertips. "So, what do we do now?"

She looked down at our hands before coming back to me, "Whatever the fuck we want."

I pulled her hand off her lap and brought it closer to me, "Whatever we do and wherever we go, it's got to be cat friendly."

Rolling her eyes, she reached across to me with her free hand, grabbing the neck of my grad gown, pulling herself toward me. The sharp minty smell of her hair, the presence in her gorgeous hazel eyes as she hung just inches from my face, paralyzed me in the moment. Her smile never left, moving in to tease mine. "You're such a nerd."

Her breath caressed my face, freezing every cell in my body. The moment our lips touched, that ever-expanding balloon burst, echoing through me like a galactic blast of energy. I ran my fingers up through the back of her hair. Her hand caressed the side of my neck, setting fireworks off in my head. Pulling her toward me, she fit her legs at my sides, my free hand running up her thigh and trapping her around her waist.

I knew this was it. The beginning of that big something.

secrets & spice

A Playlist Kinda Love Story, Side B
Coming Summer of 2023

Ashley is ready to shut the doors on her old life by embarking on a road trip with her nerdy crush, Pete. But as the dust settles, she starts to second guess her commitment to the boy who helped her escape from her abusive ex-boyfriend.

Temptation to fall back into her old, impulsive ways beckons when Ashley meets the charming Axel, putting everything she has gained with Pete at risk. Especially when Pete's eyes begin to wander too. Time is running out, and Ashley must decide if keeping Pete in the friends-with-benefits zone becomes the best or worst decision of her life.

Turn the page for an exclusive sneak peek into book 2…

ohio, tuesday, july 7th

GREMLIN PURRED in the circled nook my arms had created as I leaned on my elbows, kicking my feet in the air. The camper was small, but I couldn't ask for a cozier setup.

The entire interior was a king-sized bed. Way more than we needed, but perfect since we had a little furball sharing our space. The walls curved upward, bending into a large window that was perfect for stargazing. Both a heater and an air conditioner sat comfortably on the wall, with a cabinet just above them. We used that for the cat box, which fit miraculously. Gremlin never had a problem accessing it either, making cleaning up quick and easy. Two small shelves flanked the window and a little sill sat underneath with outlets. There was another window by the door, which is where Gremlin's cat ledge attached so he could lounge in the sun.

Outside, we had access to a small kitchenette with a sink, 2-burner stove, and a microwave. There was even a spot for a large cooler and food prep area, complete with a cabinet.

The stars were flickering between the faded tree line of our camp-site. Pete was still outside, but the insanity of the day had knocked me out. We spent the whole day settling into our camp site, which loosely translated to me giving Pete a course in camping 101. Tomorrow we'd make our first tourist stop at the Rock n' Roll Hall of Fame.

Getting into my flannel shorts and cozy tank, I unlocked my phone and scrolled through my contacts to call Dimitri. Pressing the video call button, I waited for him to answer. His giant head finally came on, moving the phone around as he slunk out of the TV blaring in his living room.

"Hold on," he said as he dashed into his small but spotless kitchen. For a college student spending most of his days running scrimmage on the field wearing a sweaty helmet, he sure knew how to keep his place tidy.

"What are you up to?" I smirked as Dimitri settled in a chair.

"Just chilling with Max. She's got some reality show on. Trust me, I'm glad you called." His eyes lit up when Gremlin's head came into view of her screen. "Aw, there's that little monster! Max already bought so much shit for that cat. I swear, she's never met him and she likes him more than me."

"Wow. Good to know how she'll be when she finally wants a kid."

Dimitri's dark eyes widened. "Don't talk like that, Ash. Don't give her any ideas."

"I wouldn't dream of it." Gremlin rubbed against my chin before settling in between my arms. "We just got to Ohio. Hitting up the Rock n' Roll Hall of Fame tomorrow."

"You gettin' me somethin', right?"

"Probably."

His perfect white teeth spread across his face in sweet satisfaction. "Nice!" He shook his head with a breathless sigh. "Man, I wish I could go with you."

"I'll send you some photos while we're there."

A few silent seconds ticked by before he shifted his tone. "So, how are things with Pete, anyway? You two… like a couple, or what?"

I peered out the window where the fire still flickered. "No, just friends, I think."

"You think?"

I held my breath, trying to decide what to say next. Dimitri wasn't always there for me, but when he was, it was always 100 percent. Which is more than I could say for my other brother, Ty, that self-centered asshole. "I don't wanna commit to anything, you know? Not after all the bullshit with Wes."

"He knows that, right?"

Pressing my lips tight, I kept the bullshit from leaking out. I couldn't think about it, let alone say it. I could talk the talk but, sometimes, it was hard to push myself to walk the walk. The last two days had been perfect so far. Just doing our thing, nothing weighing us down. But it was a lie, an illusion. I knew I couldn't keep it up, but I wanted to. How shitty did that make me? Pretty damn shitty. A user. I'd used Pete way before our first kiss. Letting myself get carried away and not respecting his boundaries. Putting him in danger with Wes without caring if he got hurt. I knew I had him hooked and I dragged him along, just like I was doing now.

Fucking bitch.

Dimitri shook his head. "Ash, don't be stupid. Look what happened with that prick, Wes."

"I know. I know. I'll… I'll tell him."

Max's face came on the screen. She was in a loose fitting tee with her hair up in a tight bun. "Ash! What's up?"

"Hey, Max."

"Enjoying the trip so far?"

"Yeah, it's going. Still got a way to go."

"You're only young once." She pulled Dimitri's ear. "Don't keep this guy too long. I don't get him to myself too often. With all his football shit."

Dimitri glanced at her. "What about your cosmetology shit?"

"Yeah, what about it?" Her pink-glossed lips landed a peck on Dimitri before she left the screen. "Talk to you later, Ash!"

With a small roll of his tongue, Dimitri raised a brow to me. "Sorry, Ash. Gotta split. Can't let that kiss go to waste."

I stuck my finger into my mouth. "Yuck, don't air out your dirty laundry in front of me. That's nasty!"

A chuckle escaped him as he leaned back in his chair. "You're right, you're right. Listen. I know you've been all over the place, take it easy on this Pete kid, okay?"

"I'll try." I waved, lifting Gremlin up so he could flap his paw goodbye. "Don't do anything I wouldn't do!"

"No chance. Talk to you later, sis."

The call ended. I swiped my phone back to the home screen. Pressing my finger on the the gallery app, I scrolled through the photos of me and Pete from our journey so far. Being stupid in the car, pumping gas, showing off like a real couple should. We looked so carefree, like nothing could have ruined the good times we were having. The thought tugged at my heart a bit.

I'd gotten too good at hiding things.

Sitting on my knees, I raised myself up to the long shelf along the top of the bed. My hand fell on a small, wooden box I had slipped up there before we left New York. Looking down on it, I felt the smooth wood against my fingers, tracing the etching of my name across the front. My dad made me this box. With a harsh breath, I lifted the lid just enough for a little artificial light to filter through. The rush of blood picked up as the knitted outline of my woven bracelet came into view. That bracelet was meant to be worn to remember my dad. It was the last gift he'd ever given me, and after he died, it was the catalyst of my self-destruction.

How could something given out of love change me so drastically and become something I never wanted to be attached to ever again?

The day I took it off and placed it in this box was so freeing. But now, staring at it in the cold wooden coffin I'd banished it to, it had never been more tempting to put back on.

The door opened, and Pete dragged himself in. I shut the box and slid it back onto the shelf as he sat on the bed to take off his shoes, dropping them on the mat before closing the door. My blood pressure slowed at the smell of campfire smoke overtaking the cabin, bringing back memories of roasting marshmallows and listening to my Dad tell scary stories by the fire.

"I need to brush up on my fire making skills."

I leaned my head in my hand and turned toward him. "You telling me you weren't a pyromaniac when you were younger?"

"Uh, no. I'm not nuts." He took off his jacket, shaking any ash free from his messy blond hair.

"Loving fire doesn't make you nuts."

"I'm assuming you've had experience with this topic?" Pete eyed me suspiciously as Gremlin bounded to him, rubbing his furry love all over Pete's extended hand.

A sly smirk graced my face. "I may have lit my living room rug on fire when I was a kid."

"I knew you were insane." Rolling across the bed, he came to rest right beside me.

I looked away from him, remembering my brother's words. *Take it easy on him*, yeah right. We would be stuck together for the entirety on this road trip. Why stir the pot and make things awkward?

"Hey." Looking up from my internal monologue, Pete held out his hand. Two white earbuds sat in his palm. "Wanna listen?"

Taking one, I popped it in my ear with a smirk. Pete took out his phone and scrolled through the plethora of music he had stored up for the trip. "Any requests?"

I shook her head. "You know what I like."

He glanced out the stargazer window, raising his eyebrows, along with his smirk. "Well, I hope this is a good choice, then." He put the earbud in and laid down under the window.

I came in close, nuzzling against his shoulder as the music churned into our ears. Laying against him, I draped my arm across his chest. The strong scent of smoke escaped from his hair. Drawing into his warmth, the cool waves of M83 made the stars dance like crystal light. Pete's arm came around me, bringing me right against him. Gremlin attempted to squeeze between us, falling over and coming to rest against my back.

I should tell him right now. Before I waited too long and convinced myself not to. But why couldn't this be enough? Maybe if my life wasn't so fucked up, it would have been. But as much as severing my ties with Wes was a defining moment in the life I was leading, it wasn't the final one. Forgetting, was it even possible? Moving on seemed like an eternity of struggle and more added bullshit.

The problem was I didn't want to move on. I wanted to stay in this bubble forever, with Pete's arms around me staring at the stars. But that was a far cry from reality. Because tomorrow, I would have to get up and live again. Another day waiting for the inevitable to happen. And I didn't even know what that inevitable was going to be.

I had to figure it out and hope like hell that I didn't screw up.

acknowledgments

Who do I thank for helping my dream come true? I never thought becoming a published author was something that would **ACTUALLY** happen to me. But it did and I am incredibly grateful to everyone who helped me along the way.

To my hubbie and kids who let me sit and write on my phone during all those insane nights in. For never saying it was a waste of time. For wanting to be apart of my journey, even when I felt it was taboo. You never once made me feel like it wasn't important.

To the amazing supporters in the writing world. My editor and cover designer, you rock! To my insta-family, the fellow writers and authors who gave me advice and cheered me on from concept to completion. I am forever grateful for finding you and I cannot wait to see where your writing journeys take you. Know I will be cheering you on from the sidelines like a mad-person the entire time.

To the music that gave this book life. I listened to countless playlists & albums while writing the words that would become Pete and Ashley's story. So thank you Timecop1983, The Midnight, Trevor Something, Kalax, Jessie Frye, W O L F C L U B, Ollie Wride, and the countless other synthwave artists who fueled my fire.

And lastly, I want to thank you, for giving my little book a chance to grace your imaginations. I hope you find joy and inspiration in these pages, as I did while writing it.

kisses & stones playlist

Here are all the songs that were referenced in the book. Please, take a listen! And check out to the official Kisses & Stones writing playlist on my YouTube channel **@d.allymusic.**

Bohemian Rhapsody - Queen
Dream Away - The Midnight
Shadowplay - Joy Division
Atmosphere - Joy Division
Lovers - Timcop1983

about the author

D. Allyson Howlett lives in a New England farm town with her husband, two boys, three house pets and four crazy chickens. She is an avid fan of all things 80's and enjoys pizza and ice cream with her family. **Kisses & Stones** is her first published novel.

thanks for reading!

*I hope you enjoyed **Kisses & Stones**!*

If you loved this book, please leave a review! It's what indie authors thrive on, so I would very much appreciate your words!

I am so excited for what the future holds for Pete and Ashley! I hope you are too! You can stay connected with me in a variety of social locations.

Find me on the inter-webs:

www.dallysonhowlett.com